To Isabelle

daisy drama club

ON TOUR

love Belinda x

written and illustrated by

belinda roberts

BEETLEHEART
PUBLISHING

www.beetleheart.co.uk

BEETLEHEART PUBLISHING

Daisy Drama Club - On Tour
was first published
in the United Kingdom in 2013
by Beetleheart Publishing.

www.daisydramaclub.co.uk

ISBN
0-9540208-8-X
978-0-9540208-8-0

www.beetleheart.co.uk

Contents

Sophie and Cressida

Lou

Alice and Wolfgang

Beaky

Susie

Harry and Hen

Abby and Pickle and Bertie

daisy drama club

... and John

To all the members
of the original

daisy drama club

Turnaround Mystery

Sophie and Cressida stared at the letter. It was written on sea-blue crinkly paper in wavy, watery writing. It said ...

To Theatrical Sensations
Miss Sophie and Miss Cressida,

Congratulations! Congratulations!
Celebrations! Celebrations!
Jubilations! Jubilations!

The fame of the fantasticalicas Daisy Drama Club has spread far and wide by someone telling someone who told someone who told someone who told *me* about you!

And so I have decided to invite the fantasticalicas Daisy Drama Club to take part in our

Seaward-on-Sea Theatre Festival!

You will perform in ...
the famous *Lady of the Waves Theatre,*
then the mysterious *Cave Theatre*
and finally ...
the spectacular *Turnaround Theatre.*
Turnaround Theatre!

As honoured guests you may camp for free at the Seaward-on-Sea lighthouse campsite! For free!

Yours in the name of lights on! Lights off! Lights on! Lights off!

Captain A J W B R Turnaround, Turnaround
Lighthouse Man
Seaward-on-Sea Lighthouse
Seaward-on-Sea

 2

PS Seaward-on-Sea lighthouse campsite is linked to the lighthouse from the land by a causeway - that is a bumpy path built on rocks. Drive across. Drive across. Just enough grass on campsite to pitch your tents.

PPS Bring plenty of tent pegs. Windy out here. Don't get blown away. Blown away!

PPPS The views are splendid! Splendid!

It was Saturday morning and Cressida was at Sophie's home, The Old Farmhouse.

Sophie and Cressie were tiptop best friends and although they were very different in *some* ways - Sophie was tall and Cressie was small and Sophie had long hair and Cressie had short hair - in *important* ways they were the same, which is what made them best friends.

Very importantly they both loved drama but because there were *no* drama clubs or theatre groups or stage schools or acting academies in their little village of Wissop whatsoever, they had

had the brilliant idea to set up their *own* club - the one and only, specially special Daisy Drama Club (or *DDC* if you are in a rush). And running a drama club and putting on plays had turned out to be even more full of thrills and spills then either of them had ever imagined.

Any minute the other members of the Daisy Drama Club would arrive - Abby, Lou, Harry, Hen, Susie, Beaky and the newest recruit, Alice.

Now the letter from the mysterious Captain Turnaround had sailed in out of the blue. It had landed splat bang wallop on The Old Farmhouse doormat that very morning.

'The DDC *on tour*! I can't believe it!'

'Who *is* Captain Turnaround?'

'How would we *get* to Seaward-on-Sea?'

'Where *is* Seaward-on-Sea?'

'First,' said Cressida, 'we should have a vote. Shall we accept Captain Turnaround's invitation or not?'

As presidents of the Daisy Drama Club, Sophie and Cressida were the only two who could make important DDC decisions. Sometimes they just agreed. Sometimes they had a vote. To go or not to go on tour was an important decision so they had a vote: a hand in the air was a *yes;* no hands in the air was a *no.* The girls shut their eyes and when they opened them again both had a hand in the air. That was a *yes.*

'Yippee!' cried Sophie.

'Extraordinary times like this mean extraordinary actions are needed. We need to hold an Extraordinary Emergency Urgent Meeting,' said Cressida, whose aunt was an important businesswoman so Cressie knew all about Extraordinary Emergency Urgent Meetings. 'We need an Extraordinary Emergency Urgent Meeting to tell the Daisy Drama Club members that we are off on tour!'

Sophie's bedroom was the DDC headquarters. On her door was a handwritten sign that said ...

ddc hq

In her bedroom, as well as a bed and books and teddies and posters and clothes and shoes and a mirror and all the normal stuff, was a large black box with ddc office written on the front in gold letters.

It also said ...

private!

top secret!

hands off!

Inside the office all sorts of important DDC items were kept including:

✻ five pieces of paper with *Daisy Drama Club* written at the top.

✻ fifteen pieces of paper waiting to have *Daisy Drama Club* written at the top.

✻ eleven postcards with *Daisy Drama Club* written on one side.

✻ seven postcards cut out waiting to have *Daisy Drama Club* written on one side.

✻ two black pens.

✻ 6 ✻

✳ a yellow crayon.

✳ two DDC membership application forms.

✳ six DDC membership application forms filled in.

✳ one DDC membership application form filled in but with *ON TRIAL (Alice)* written across the front.

✳ a folder that said *Plays Performed* and inside the folder were five tickets and one programme for *A Christmas Carol* and two tickets and three programmes for *Red Riding Hood*.

✳ one *Things To Do* notebook.

✳ a button.

✳ two humbugs.

✳ a cotton reel.

✳ a pair of scissors.

✳ some string.

✳ more string, various lengths.

✳ Sophie's maths homework book.

'There it is!' said Sophie, surprised. 'How did my maths homework get there? Miss Guffy went super berserk when I didn't hand it in on Friday!'

But Cressie was not interested in the maths book or Miss Guffy. She had already got out the postcards and was busy writing out messages in black pen. This is what she wrote ...

Extraordinary Emergency Urgent Meeting
to talk about ...
the Turnaround Mystery Invitation
to go ON TOUR.
Saturday 10.00am at The Barn Theatre
and not later!

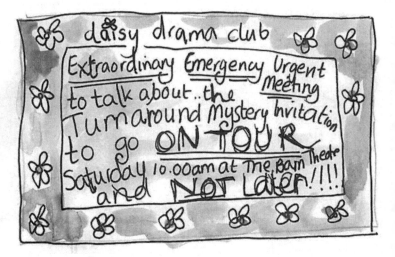

She turned the postcard over and wrote '*To Abby*'.
'We need six more - one for everyone - that's Harry, Hen, Beaky, Lou, Susie and Alice.'

'And one for John. We would need him to come too.'

John was Sophie's brother who was as crazy about insects and spiders or anything tiny with lots of legs as Sophie and Cress were crazy about drama. John was the DDC lighting director which he enjoyed as it meant he could sit up in the lighting gallery of The Barn Theatre which was old and wooden and crawling with creepy crawlies.

Clip! Clop!

Clip! Clop!

Clip! Clop!

'Oh no!' said Cressida alarmed. 'That's Abby on Pickle here already! Hurry! Hurry!'

Cressida's hand flew across the postcard, writing at top speed.

'Leaping liquorice!' came a cry from outside. There was no mistaking Harry and Hen, the twins with the bright red hair, big smiles, freckles and massive front teeth. 'Pickle - love your plaits!'

'Thanks,' said Abby, speaking for her pony, Pickle. 'I nearly finished doing them. I'm practising plaiting his mane for Wissop show but I ran out of time so I've still got about four to do!'

9

'We'll finish off,' said Harry twirling round her own plaits.

'We've had lots of practice,' added Hen, twirling round *her* plaits.

The girls started plaiting the remainder of Pickle's mane while Abby tried to hold him still. But Pickle tossed his head up and down. He did not like being at the hairdressers.

'Bye darling! Kiss! Kiss!' came the piercing voice of Mrs Theodora Whistle-White.

'Oh everyone's arriving!' said Cressida writing faster than ever. 'That's Susie!'

Shy little fluffy haired Susannah-Sue Whistle-White had been dropped off by her star struck mother, Mrs Theodora Whistle-White.

'Lou,' they heard Susie - who was practising being brave - say to Lou who had come along with Beaky and Alice and was patting Wolfgang, Alice's beloved hairy grey wolfhound, 'I hope I can be your make-up athithtant for the next play. I have been practithing and practithing with my mother'th make-up and managed to turn myself into a fabulouth tiger! Grrr!'

Wolfgang growled back.

'Oh thorry Wolfgang. I didn't mean to frighten you!' said Susie, frightened herself.

But Wolfgang had spotted Lollipop, Abby's

sheepdog and had dashed over to nip his ear. Lollipop bit back and soon the two dogs were racing round and round the maple tree in the middle of the yard with Abby and Alice chasing after them.

Upstairs in the DDC HQ Cressie and Sophie were still writing out the Extraordinary Emergency Urgent Meeting notes.

'Hurry!' urged Cress. '*We* mustn't be late!'

Sophie had nearly finished her first note when she had a thought. 'Wait a sec Cress. Everyone is here anyway so why do we need to write out these emergency notes?'

'Because it *is* an emergency - and we need everyone to understand how important this is.'

Sophie wasn't convinced but carried on writing notes anyway. To save time she wrote ...

EEUM to discuss the TMI to go OT
Sat 10.00 TBT and not

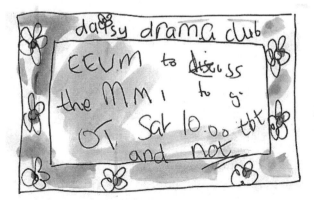

Finished, the girls dashed downstairs and out into the yard where all the members of the Daisy Drama Club were still milling around trying to stop Lollipop and Wolfgang fighting and trying to stop Pickle eating the flowers and trying to stop Bertie, Abby's pet mouse, from getting lost *in* the flowers.

Cressida and Sophie hurriedly gave out all the Extraordinary Emergency Urgent Meeting notes and raced into The Barn Theatre. Everyone read their note and ran in afterwards and sat down on the little chairs that Sophie's Uncle Max had given them before their very first performance.

Susie read her note and looked anxious.

'I jutht don't underthtand thith one little bit,' she said frowning. ' *d d c e e u m to discuth the m m i to go o t. That 10.00 t b t and not.* Ith it a mythtery code or thomething?'

'Sorry,' mumbled Sophie, 'but we were in a hurry.'

'This is an Extraordinary Emergency Urgent Meeting to discuss a mysterious letter that came this morning,' explained Cressida.

Sophie read out the letter from Captain Turnaround.

'Leaping liquorice!' said Harry flicking her long red plaits round and round. 'We're famous!'

'Leaping liquorice!' added Hen, flicking her red plaits round and round. 'Camping!'

'Who is Captain Turnaround?'

'The person who wrote the letter.'

'Where is Seaward-on-Sea?'

'Somewhere near the sea.'

'How do you put up a tent?'

'Not very easily.'

'Why is it a tour?'

'Because we *tour* from Wissop to Seaward-on-Sea.'

'Then we *tour* from one theatre to the next.'

'Can I bring Wolfgang?'

'If you bring Wolfgang can I bring Pickle?'

'Do they have different sorts of spiders by the sea?'

(That was John calling down from the lighting gallery).

'What will we eat?'

(That was John again).

'What play will we do?'

It was this final question that brought a sudden halt to the discussion. It was a pretty important question that needed a pretty important answer.

What play would they do?

Sophie and Cressida had no idea.

Then Susannah-Sue Whistle-White, who much preferred to be called Susie, suddenly screeched, 'Oh! I've had a bolt from the blue! A lightning flath! A crath of inthpiration! We should do a play about the theethide thinth we are going to the theethide!'

'You are a genius Susie!' said Cressida.

Susie beamed with pride and said modestly, 'Oh, thometimeth theethe flatheth of geniuth do come to me!'

'But does anybody know a good seasidy sort of play?' asked Sophie.

Everyone looked blank.

There was only one thing for it thought Sophie and Cressida thinking the very same thing at the very same moment, as only best friends do: *ask Beaky to write a play specially for the tour*.

'Beaky ...' said Cressida.

'Beaky ...' said Sophie, 'would you like to ... with the help of Grandpa Albert ...?'

'... write a play ...' finished Beaky, tapping her nose and closing her eyes. 'Already I can see the sea crashing against rocks, fish and seagulls, sandy beaches, a lighthouse.'

Beaky opened her eyes and beamed.

'Grandpa Albert and I would be honoured!'

'That's it then,' said Sophie delighted. 'We have a play - or nearly a play. Now all we have to do is persuade our parents that going on tour is a brilliant idea!'

A Lighthouse Legend

Luckily all the parents and grandparents and uncles and aunts *did* think going on tour was a brilliant idea. Mrs Theodora Whistle-White thought it a *sensational* step forward in Susie's acting career.

'You see darling!' she cooed, 'your fabulous performance as the leading lady in the Daisy Drama Club's *Red Riding Hood* has bought fame and fortune to the DDC! You *must* go! Oscars are beckoning!'

'But I have never been away before,' said Susie. The idea of going away made her feel trembly. 'I'll be homethick. I know I will. Jutht thinking about it ith making me feel homethick now and I'm thtill at home!'

A large tear fell down Susie's cheek.

Mrs Theodora Whistle-White hugged her little daughter. 'You won't be homesick! You'll be so busy performing!'

But Mrs Theodora Whistle-White, whilst ambitious, also adored her little girl and the thought of being parted from her even for only a few days made her feel trembly too. A tear made its way slowly through the thick layers of make-up on Mrs Theodora Whistle-White's cheek and landed gently, like a soft white snowflake, in Susie's fluffy hair.

Meanwhile Beaky had rushed round to tell her Grandpa Albert the exciting news.

'A tour! How fantasticalicas!'

'That's odd!' said Beaky. 'Captain Turnaround said *we* were fantasticalicas in his letter. How would he know your special word? Do you *know* him Grandpa?'

'Captain Turnaround from Seaward-on-Sea? Let me think ...' Grandpa Albert tapped his nose thoughtfully. 'No. Never, ever, ever, ever heard of him. And that is for definite.'

'That's odd then, times two. *One* that he has heard of *us* and *two* that he has used your special word. Somebody must have told somebody who told somebody who told somebody who told Captain Turnaround.'

Grandpa Albert thought for a moment.

'I did tell my sister, Ethel - that is your Great Aunt Ethel - when she came to stay that you had done a fantasticalicas play but she lives right at the top of

England and Seaward-on-Sea is right at the bottom so it couldn't be her. Now what fantasticalicas play are you going to do this time?'

'That's why I have come to see you. The DDC has asked us to write a special on tour script!'

'Another script! Yippee!' cried Grandpa Albert.

'Yes. And Susie had such a good idea,' added Beaky tapping her nose in excitement. 'It came to her like a bolt from the blue! A lightning flash! A crash of inspiration! We should do a story about the seaside since we are going to the seaside!'

'Fantasticalicas again!' said Albert.

'But,' said Beaky, 'I have been thinking and thinking about what the story could actually be about and I haven't been able to think of a single thing - apart from a lighthouse and a light going round and round and then ideas start to go round and round in my head and I always come back to the same place - nowhere.'

'Beaky! I have the very thing!' said Albert diving into an ancient chest. 'I have got all sorts of stories and writings and jottings and diaries and poems in here that I have written over the years.'

Bits of paper covered in writing flew everywhere. At last Grandpa Albert exclaimed, 'Ah ha! Here we are. This story was inspired by my great, great, great,

great, great and lots more greats grandpa who was of course your great, great, great, great, great and lots *lots* more greats grandpa.'

Beaky was thrilled. More relations to get to know. Family life at Beaky's home was as dull as a dried up doormat. She had no brothers or sisters. Not even one small annoying one. Her parents were goggle-eyed, super-brainy genius professors, always working in

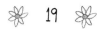

their dusty studies and didn't notice her at all. They would not even notice if she went on tour without telling them. The house was always deadly silent. Beaky had to tiptoe about so the important professors and their important work was never, ever disturbed.

Grandpa Albert was just as clever as her parents but he was lively and Beaky's best friend. He had had *hundreds* of brothers and sisters, as well as Ethel. He was the oldest but his childhood was so long ago he could hardly remember who was who. What he *did* remember was that it was always noisy and crowded when he was growing up. How Beaky *longed* for some noise and crowds at her home.

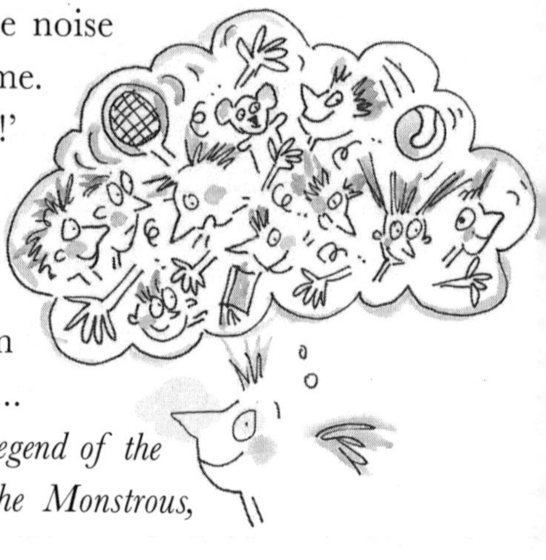

'Aha! Here we are!' cried Albert.

Grandpa Albert handed Beaky a little hand made book. On the front was written ...

The Extraordinary Legend of the Lighthouse Man and the Monstrous, Monster of the Deep.

'I'll read it to you down by the stream,' said Grandpa Albert. 'It's one of those stories that needs a watery background.'

So Beaky and Grandpa Albert went down to the stream at the bottom of the garden and sat down on the mossy bank. They took off their shoes and with their feet dangling in the water, Grandpa Albert read to Beaky.

And this is what he read ...

THE EXTRAORDINARY LEGEND OF THE LIGHTHOUSE MAN AND THE MONSTROUS MONSTER OF THE DEEP

Once upon a time there was a rocky island. The island was surrounded by jagged rocks that thrust up out of the sea and the biggest of all these rocks was the island itself. Passing ships were ripped to pieces, torn to shreds and smashed to smithereens by these sharp rocks and many sailor s lives were lost – that is until one man was brave enough and tough enough and hardy enough to man a lighthouse on the rocky island. He was so brave and tough and hardy that the fact that there was NO lighthouse on the rocky island did not matter to him.

Oh no! He would be the lighthouse and spend his days with a light on his head turning and turning and saving lives. It was a sacrifice he was willing to make even if to begin with he felt dizzy.

His two children who lived with him on the rocky island were equally resourceful.

The eldest was a girl called Angelica who had an inventions box and invented all sorts of useful gadgets to make their life on the island more comfortable.

The youngest was a boy called Cornet who loved ice-creams but had never had one. He spent his time fishing but the only thing

inventions box

he ever caught was evil smelling stinking eels which swarmed in the waters below and which were slippery and slimy and disgustingly horrible to eat.

It was a rough, tough existence.

But what the lighthouse man and his brave and bold children did not know was that in the swirling, whirling waters below the rocky island lurked not just tiddly little eels but the biggest, most monstrously monstrous eel that ever existed. This monster eel was becoming more and more angry with Cornet for catching and eating all the other eels — his brothers and sisters and uncles and aunts and grannies and grandpas! And an angry eel is a dangerous eel. This angry, dangerous eel wanted ...

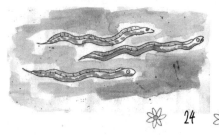

REVENGE!!!

So because Cornet had eaten the monster eel's brothers and sisters and uncles and aunts and grannies and grandpas the monster eel decided to EAT Cornet!

That seemed fair.

The eel was sly as well as slimy. He knew Cornet longed for an ice-cream. So the evil eel put on a straw hat and long coat and disguised himself as an ice-cream seller. He landed on the rocky island pushing an ice-cream trolley filled with delicious ice-creams.

But not any old ice-creams! OH NO!

These were magic ice-creams that with one lick would turn you into a fish!

Angelica – who was very intelligent and would grow up to be a Professor of inventions with lots of letters after her name including …

A.B.C.D.E.F.G.H.I.J.K.L.M.N.O.P.Q.R.T.U.V.W.X.Y.Z.

… which is nearly every letter you can think of – immediately suspected something fishy going on.

Cornet just saw delicious ice-creams and fell for the trap …

hook …

… line …

… and sinker.

One lick and the magic started to work. Cornet grew scales!

… he grew a flipperty, flapperty tail!

… his eyes went goggly and glassy!

… he turned into a fish boy!

'HA! HA! HA!' laughed the monster eel and whisked away the fish boy into the deep seas.

Angelica screamed and wailed and then pulled herself together. She invented a diving suit for herself and a Brother Nit Wit Detector Kit to track Cornet down and dived under the waves.

The poor lighthouse man, turning and turning, missed the tragic events until it was too late. His children had disappeared! Vanished! Pop! Evaporated into a spray of seawater. Through his tears he saw a left over ice-cream and could not resist a lick to drown his sorrows. The effect was immediate!

He grew scales!

... he grew a flipperty, flapperty tail!

... his eyes went goggly and glassy!

... he turned into a lighthouse man fish!

He slithered and slipped into the water and with the light still turning on his head he swam off into the salty seas.

Meanwhile the eel was just about to eat Cornet when he caught sight of the beautiful Princess Crabella, a little crab, who lived in the delightful green frondy underwater kingdom  with her father, King Fathom-Five-Deep and her mother Queen Scuttlebucket.

With all his relations eaten the eel was lonely as well as angry and decided to kidnap and marry Crabella. They would eat Cornet together at their wedding feast!

So while Princess Crabella and her father King Fathom-Five-Deep waited for the arrival of Crabella s fine fiance, the lobster Prince Lobalot, an ice-cream seller came into their swirling, whirling underwater frondy garden. This time the ice-creams would send you to sleep.

'Oh my favourite!' cried the King choosing a stickleback cornetto ice-cream. The King took one lick and promptly started snoring.

'HA! HA! HA!' cried the monstrous monster throwing off his ice-cream seller disguise and snatching Princess Crabella. You will be my bride! HA! HA! HA!

The evil eel swept the terrified Princess Crabella away and locked her in his lair with Cornet.

Meanwhile Queen Scuttlebucket found the king asleep and Princess Crabella gone! But Queen Scuttlebucket was no ordinary queen. She had a big big secret. She was secretly the famous,

sensational, brave and bold Super Queen!

'Super Queen! Super Queen! Kind to the good! Horrid to the mean!'

Immediately she set off on her mission to rescue

Crabella. Her supersonic hearing alerted her to the bleeping from Angelica's Brother Nit Wit Detector Kit which led them to an evil, stinking cave. In a dark dim corner, to their delight, they saw Cornet and Princess Crabella locked up in lobster pots. Joy! Victory! Then disaster! The monster eel slily crept up on Angelica and Super Queen and was just about to entrap them in his evil coils when Super Queen showed what she was made of and tied him up, hook, line and sinker – and freed Cornet and Crabella!

But there was no time for celebration yet.

With the evil eel in tow, Angelica, Cornet, Princess Crabella and Super Queen swam back to King Fathom-Five-Deep's castle. Just in time to stop Prince Lobalot giving up and going home!

Just as everything seemed to have worked out perfectly the monster eel wriggled out of his hook, line and sinker and grabbed Princess Crabella!

All seemed lost ...

... until the lighthouse man fish swam in. The turning turning light on the lighthouse man fish's head hypnotised the eel. He fell into a trance! The brilliant Angelica took her chance and made the eel promise to free Princess Crabella to marry Lobalot and in return they would never catch eels again and the monster eel must visit them every day so he would not be lonely any more. The monster agreed. Victorious Angelica, Cornet, the lighthouse man and the monstrous eel swam back to the rocky island.

After that the monster eel kept his promise and visited the rocky island every day. He became quite a tourist attraction and the tourists paid in picnic hampers so there was no need for Cornet to catch eels any more — they had much more interesting things to eat.

And the lighthouse man kept on turning and turning and saving lives so everyone lived happily ever after.

The End

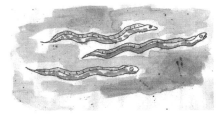

Beaky threw her arms round her grandpa. 'That was funny! Frightening! Fabulous! It'll make a fantasticalicas play! Was the lighthouse man your great, great, great, great and lots of greats grandpa?'

'Yes. And *your* great, great, great, great, great and lots of greats grandpa who really was in a ship that sailed across to England and really did go down on a rocky island. Everyone was lost except for your great, great, great, great, great and lots of greats grandpa and his little girl and boy. So he decided there and then to make it safer to sail to England and was a lighthouse on the island himself until he had enough money to build a real lighthouse. So like all legends there is some truth in it. Now we need to turn the legend into a play about the legend.'

Grandpa Albert brought his ancient typewriter outside. With the babbling of the brook to inspire them they wrote a fantasticalicas play which they called *The Lighthouse Man and the Monster of the Deep*.

A Fishy Cast

At the next meeting of the Daisy Drama Club Sophie and Cressida were anxious. Would Beaky have a play? When Beaky burst into The Barn Theatre and triumphantly handed the best friends a bundle of scripts they leapt out of their chairs in delight!

'Beaky! You superstar!'

Immediately the DDC read the play through.

'That wath a fabulouth fishy adventure Beaky,' said Susie when they had finished. 'You're thou clever.'

'We did have some help from my great, great, great, great, great and lots of greats grandpa,' replied Beaky modestly.

'Oh I didn't know Grandpa Albert wath that old,' said Susie, her eyes wide in amazement.

Before Beaky could explain Abby interrupted.

'I just don't understand how the Brother Nit Wit Detector Kit would work. How could Angelica go

❀ 33 ❀

underwater and thinking about it, how could eating an ice-cream turn Cornet into a fish?'

Harry and Hen rolled their eyes.

'Leaping liquorice. Try and use your imagination just a teeny weeny bit,' said Harry.

'Leaping liquorice. I think it's a brill story,' added Hen. 'Lots of magic and mystery and action!'

Abby still looked puzzled.

'Abby, it's based on a legend which means something real happened then lots of extra bits got added on which might or might not be true,' explained Cressie trying to apply what she had been learning about Greek legends at school.

'Who will be who?' asked Alice. 'I hope I get a good part!'

Sophie and Cressida exchanged glances. Alice had only just joined the DDC before the *Red Riding Hood* performance and was still ON TRIAL.

'Shall we vote?' whispered Sophie.

Cressida nodded.

They closed their eyes. When they opened their eyes both had a hand in the air. A definite *yes*. Alice was a proper member of the DDC at last.

'Everyone will have a good part,' said Sophie. 'And that includes you Alice. Welcome to the DDC.'

Alice beamed in delight. 'Do I get a badge?'

34

'A badge?'

'Yes. Every good club has a club badge.'

'We don't have badges yet but that's a good idea. What do you think Sophie?'

Sophie waved her arm in the air. It wasn't exactly an official vote but it was good enough. Cress and Sophie had made the decision together which was the vitally important thing.

Cressida wrote *badges* on her *Things To Do List (2)*

'Here is a list of characters,' said Beaky, 'but it is up to Sophie and Cressida to actually cast the play.'

Beaky handed over the list to Sophie and Cressida. There were nine characters, one each.

They were ...

Merman - a mysterious, floaty narrator

Lachlan the Lighthouse Man
- the lighthouse man who is a lighthouse

Angelica - a girl, a genius and an inventor

Cornet - a fisher boy who only catches eels

Maximus the Monster Eel
- an evil monstrous monster eel

Princess Crabella - a delightfully pretty crab

Prince Lobalot - a lobster, engaged to Crabella

King Fathom-Five-Deep - Crabella's dozy dad

Queen Scuttlebucket and Super Queen
- Crabella's mother who turns into Super Queen

❀ 35 ❀

Casting was a delicate matter which had to be done in top secret otherwise chaos broke out.

'We'll be back in a minute,' said Cressida and she and Sophie raced up to the DDC HQ for an Emergency Casting Session.

'I think you should be Angelica, Cress. You would be perfect,' said Sophie bouncing up and down on her bed, hardly able to concentrate she was so excited at the prospect of another play.

'And Susie is definitely Princess Crabella!' added Cressida bouncing up and down for inspiration.

'Alice should be Maximus the Monster Eel.'

Boing! Boing! Boing!

'And there is something forgetful about Abby that reminds me of King Fathom-Five-Deep.'

Boing! Boing! Boing!

'You would be very funny as Queen Scuttlebucket, Sophie, especially when she turns into Super Queen.'

Boing! Boing! Boing!

'Lou could be the Merman. She would like the floaty costume.'

Boing! Boing! Boing!

'Which leaves Beaky as Lachlan the Lighthouse Man, which is good as she is tall.'

Boing! Boing! Boing!

'But what about Harry?'

'Prince Lobalot!'
'Agreed?'
'Agreed!'
Boing! Boing! Boing!

Sophie got out a big black pen and a large piece of paper from the DDC office and wrote ...

Merman – Lou
Lachlan the Lighthouse Man – Beaky
Angelica – Cressida
Cornet – Abby
Maximus the Monster Eel – Alice
Princess Crabella – Susie
Prince Lobalot – Harry
King Fathom-Five-Deep – Hen
Queen Scuttlebucket – Sophie

Directors – Sophie and Cressida
Prompt – Beaky
Wardrobe and Make-up – Lou
Wardrobe and Make-up Assistant – Susie
Scenery – Alice
Props – Harry and Hen
Lighting – John

CAST LIST

Merman ... Lou Man
Lachlan the lighthouse ... Beaky
Angelica ... Cressie
Cornet ... Abby
Maximus the monster Eel ... Alice
Princess Crabella ... Susie
Prince Lobalot ... Harry
King Fathom-Five-Deep ... Hen
Queen Scuttlebucket ... Sophie
Directors: Sophie and Cress, Prompt-Beaky
Wardrobe-Make-up Lou, Susie(assistant)
Scenery Alice, Props Harry and Hen, Lighting ... John

The presidents of the **DDC** raced back down to The Barn Theatre. They pinned the cast list up on the barn door and crossed their fingers and toes.

Would anyone complain?

Would anyone cry?

The DDC crowded round.

'Yeeeeeessssssssssssssssssss!' yelled Alice. 'I'm Maximus the Monster Eel! I love playing the baddy!'

'Everyone else happy?' ventured Cressida.

'Congratulationth Beaky,' said Susie. 'You are Lachlan the Lighthouth Man. That meanth you will have to turn round and round and round and round on thtage. I hope you will not get dithy and fall off into the lap of people on the front row.'

Beaky tapped her nose thoughtfully. Perhaps she should try out continuous turning before accepting the part. Beaky turned round and round and round and round. And so did everyone else. Soon everyone else felt whirly, twirly, dizzy, fizzy and quite unable to stand up. Everyone wibbled and wobbled apart from Beaky who was still turning and turning and turning.

'Ooooh Beaky,' said Susie. 'You're tho clever at turning. You are the only one who could pothibly be the lighthouth man!'

Beaky smiled and tapped her nose.

'Turning must be in the blood,' she said, delighted that turning, as well as writing, was something she was obviously quite good at!

Rehearsals

The next two weeks saw intense activity. Daily rehearsals took place in The Barn Theatre and when they were not rehearsing all the DDC were busy getting ready in other theatrical ways ...

* Beaky made tiny tweaks to the script ...
* Lou spent her evenings whizzing up spectacular costumes on her sewing machine ...
* Susie sorted out the muddle that was the make-up box ...
* Harry and Hen, without much help from Abby, collected all the props together and made a splendid Brother Nit Wit Detector Kit out of tubes and boxes and whirly things and odd bits and strange pieces ...

✳ Alice painted posters and decorated them
   brilliantly with lobsters and lighthouses ...

✳ ... and Sophie and Cressida made
   endless *Things to Do Lists* ...

Everyone was super excited about going on tour.
Everyone that is, except Abby.

Susie, who was very sensitive, noticed that Abby
looked distracted and unhappy.

'What ith the matter Abby?' asked Susie just before
they had yet another run through of the play. Bertie,
Abby's white mouse who went everywhere with her,

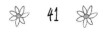

was peeping out of Abby's top pocket. 'Ith it Bertie? Ith he poorly?'

'No. It's Pickle,' said Abby in a shaky voice. 'I just don't want to leave him behind when we go on tour. I can take Bertie of course, and Alice is taking Wolfgang, and Lollipop has to stay behind to look after the sheep because he is a sheepdog. Only Pickle will be left out. He will be so lonely without me!'

Susie was still worried herself about being homesick so she could understand that Abby would be homesick for Pickle and Pickle would be homesick for Abby.

Abby started crying again and Susie, because she couldn't think of anything to say, started crying too.

Sophie was calling, 'Scene one! Scene one!'

Abby sighed and took her position on stage as Cornet the fisher boy.

Beaky was already on stage turning and turning. She was a natural lighthouse man.

```
LACHLAN THE LIGHTHOUSE MAN
    I know it sounds queer,
    But I'm perfectly happy here
    Going round and round, hearing the sound
    Of the sea and the cries of the gulls.
    Being a lighthouse man with no lighthouse
    On this rocky island location
    May be strange, but it's my vocation!
```

Cressida was Angelica busy inventing a hat with a flap that held a map and a tap. She glanced across at Abby who looked impressively dismal as Cornet who was fishing and still only catching eels.

ANGELICA *(impatiently)*
    Caught anything Cornet?

CORNET
    Only more slimy, slippery eels.

ANGELICA
    Really Cornet! More eels.
    All our meals are eels.
    Imagine how it feels
    To be filled from your head to your heels
    With slippery, slimy
    Wibberly, wobbly,
    Disgustingly horribly
    Slimy eels!

Just then there was a 'Poop! Poop!'

Uncle Max, who loved everything theatrical, and his beautiful wife Millie with her lovely long blond curly hair, blue eyes, pink cherry lips and dimples when she smiled, drove into the yard in Max's old banger.

They hopped out and popped into The Barn Theatre. Uncle Max had offered to drive the DDC down to Seaward-on-Sea in the school minibus and wanted to come and see how rehearsals were going. Susie, peeping out from backstage, spotted him and her heart skipped a beat. Inspired by Angelica and her inventions and still thinking about Abby and Pickle she sneaked out from backstage and over to Uncle Max and whispered a brilliant idea in his ear.

It *was* a brilliant idea and Uncle Max agreed!

Stormy Start!

The day of the tour arrived.

Very, very early in the morning, when it was really still night time and the moon and stars were out, the DDC and DDC parents and Grandpa Albert, who was in his pyjamas and dressing gown, gathered in the yard at The Old Farmhouse.

Best friends Sophie and Cressida were ticking off the items on Cressida's very, very long *Things To Take on Tour List*. The very, very long *Things To Take on Tour List* said ...

PROPS

- inventions box
- Brother Nit Wit Detector Kit
- fishing rod
- bucket
- hat with a map and a tap
- hook, line and sinker
- ice-cream trolley
- ice-creams menu
- the ice-creams as on menu

... they had a quick look at the ice-cream menu ...

... and then went back to the very, very long list ...

SCENERY

- rocks for island
- coral
- shells
- seaweed
- giant shell bench
- lobster pot
- fish bones
    (remains)
- submarine suit
- book
- picnic hampers

LIGHTS

- red spotlight
- green spotlight

COSTUMES

- DDC Costume Book
- merman floaty
seaweedy (Merman)

- lighthouse man striped costume (LM)
- shorts (Cornet)
- fisherman s jumper (Cornet)
- cap (Cornet)
- boots (Cornet)
- shorts (Angelica)
- fisherman s jumper (Angelica)
- boots (Angelica)
- crown (King FF)
- tail (King FF)
- cloak (King FF)
- fins (King FF)
- crown (Q S)
- tail (Q S)
- seaweed (Q S)
- shell necklace (PC)
- cloak (SQ)
- dress (PC)
- Pincers (PC)
- Pincers (PL)
- black all in one (eel)

MAKE-UP BOX

- full of make-up
- make-up mirror 
- Lou's BBC make-up instruction manual

CAMPING

- tents x 5
- kettle
- stove
- ground sheets

EVERYONE TO ALSO BRING

- sleeping bag 
- pillow
- blanket
- cuddly
- dinner plate
- side plate
- bowl
- mug
- knife

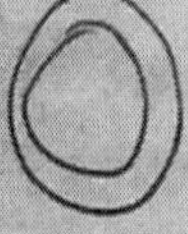

- fork
- spoon
- teaspoon
- lunchbox
- tea towel
- soap
- shampoo
- towel
- wellies
- sunhat
- pyjamas

FOR THE BEACH

- bucket
- spade
- ball
- towel
- swimming costume
- cricket bat
- boules
- flags

(no buy them there)

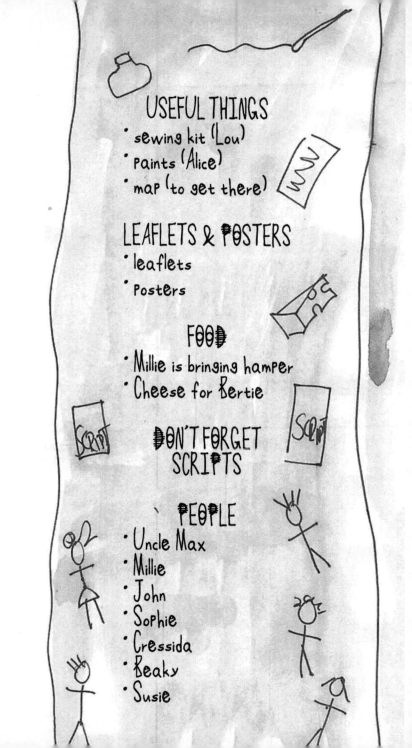

USEFUL THINGS
- sewing kit (Lou)
- paints (Alice)
- map (to get there)

LEAFLETS & POSTERS
- leaflets
- posters

FOOD
- Millie is bringing hamper
- Cheese for Bertie

DON'T FORGET
SCRIPTS

PEOPLE
- Uncle Max
- Millie
- John
- Sophie
- Cressida
- Beaky
- Susie

- Harry
- Hen
- Abby
- Lou
- Alice

PETS

- Bertie
- Wolfgang

'I think that is everything,' said Cressie doubtfully.

'I think it will just have to be,' said Sophie. 'If we don't go now we might miss our first performance which is today! But where is Uncle Max and the minibus?'

'And what is the matter with Abby?'

Abby had ridden Pickle up to The Old Farmhouse, and now the moment to part was getting closer she could not bear it. Her face was buried in Pickle's mane and she was hugging him tightly. Pickle, meanwhile, was happily nosing about in Abby's

 53

packed breakfast which she had unwisely left on the ground just in reach.

At that very moment Uncle Max and his enchanting wife Millie with her lovely long blond curly hair, blue eyes, pink cherry lips and dimples when she smiled, drove into the yard of The Old Farmhouse. For once Uncle Max was not driving his old banger. Instead he was driving the school minibus.

But it didn't *look* like the school minibus.

It looked like the ...

Daisy Drama Club *On Tour* tour minibus

On the sides was painted ...

Daisy Drama Club On Tour!
The Lighthouse Man and the Monster of the Deep

And in all the gaps and on the roof and the bonnet and the doors there were pictures of daisies ... and stripy lighthouses ... and scaly fish ... and salty seaweed ... and barnacled lobster pots ... and crusty crabs ... and whirly, twirly shells ...

On the roof was tied a massive trunk to stuff in as many props and bits of scenery and costumes as possible. Everything else would go inside.

'What do you think?' cried Uncle Max leaping out.

'It's fantasticalicas!' said Beaky.

'Did you paint thoth pictureth yourthelf?' Susie asked in wonder.

'Oh no!' said Uncle Max. 'It was Alice. I said that I was picking up the minibus yesterday and if she wanted to decorate it she could.'

'Alith!' said Susie. 'You're tho clever!'

'Thank you,' said Alice. 'I've also made these.'

Alice had a little tin with her. She opened the lid.

 55

It was full of DDC badges, all handmade by Alice.

Sophie and Cressida looked surprised. They had got badges on their *Things To Do List (2)* but Alice was one step ahead. Should she have designed badges without asking them, as presidents, first? But as Sophie and Cress both knew without asking each other, they had so many things to think about that perhaps they should just be grateful.

'Thanks Alice, those are brilliant,' said Sophie graciously. Cressida agreed.

'Leaping liquorice! Tiptop!' said Harry and Hen together.

Alice handed the tin round and everyone chose a badge, just like you might choose a sweet.

A sob from inside the tour minibus and the sound of someone trying to stifle their cries in a large handkerchief distracted them. It was Millie.

'Oh dear! I am sorry,' said Millie. 'I'm just so, so, so sad at having to leave my creaky old people.'

And with that Millie started crying again.

Uncle Max had volunteered to drive the DDC down to Seaward-on-Sea but he could not bear to leave his lovely wife Millie so Millie said she would come too. Millie and Uncle Max lived at Bluebell House where they looked after five creaky old people of whom Millie was very fond. This was the first time she had been away but the five creaky old people had insisted she should go and they absolutely promised they would not get up to mischief. And after all, they were in good hands as Grandpa Albert had promised to look after them.

'I've promised I will look after them and I will,' said Grandpa Albert. 'They wanted to come and wave you off but they are far too old and creaky to be up in the middle of the night. Right now they are all tucked up fast asleep in their beds at Bluebell House so don't you worry.'

There was a cough from a nearby hedgerow.

'My!' said Millie. 'That sounded just like ... no silly me. I must be imagining things.'

Millie did not spot five pairs of eyes peeping out from the hedgerow. The five creaky old people never liked to miss out on anything!

'All aboard!' called Uncle Max. 'Why don't you sing some of your sea shanties to us on the way to cheer you up Millie.'

'Shall I dearest Max?' said Millie cheering up immediately. 'There is nothing like a sea shanty to put you in a jolly mood!' And she smiled her lovely smile showing off her delightful dimples.

The parents and grandparents and uncles and aunts who had gathered to see the DDC off, started hugging and kissing the children - none more vigorously than Mrs Theodora Whistle-White.

'I'm missing you already my darling girl,' said Mrs Theodora Whistle-White hugging Susie tightly in her big furry coat.

'Don't worry. I will be quite alright,' came Susie's muffled voice from within the coat. 'Although of courth I will mith you!'

'Oh Susannah-Sue, you are so brave!' cooed Mrs Whistle-White, sighing and wishing her daughter didn't have to pay such a high price for stardom.

The tour minibus was loaded up and ready to go.

Abby had Bertie in her pocket but was still hugging Pickle.

'Come on, Abby,' said Uncle Max. 'Time to go. Come along Pickle.'

Uncle Max led the surprised Pickle up a ramp and into the back of the tour minibus and shut the door.

'Well,' he said to the incredulous Abby, 'you wouldn't have wanted to leave him behind would you? Susie said you would miss him so we reckoned there was just enough room to squeeze him in. Look!'

Uncle Max had made a little stable at the back of the tour minibus and had even hung up a haynet and put a little sign saying *Pickle on Tour* to make Pickle feel part of the show.

Abby nearly fainted with joy! She threw all her stuff into the minibus, then threw her arms around Uncle Max and around Susie and leapt aboard.

At that very moment it started to rain. A few drops soon turned into a great downpour then a tremendous torrent. The parents ran for shelter in The Barn Theatre. Uncle Max hopped into the driving seat, with Millie in the front passenger seat and John, clasping the map, squeezed between them. Uncle Max tooted the horn and with much waving, hooting, crying and shouting and whizzing of windscreen wipers they were off ...

... THE TOUR HAD BEGUN!

A Wild and Windy Journey

After the DDC had sung five of Millie's sea shanties, eaten four bags of sweets and Wolfgang had wolfed down Uncle Max's box of shortbread the DDC fell asleep.

The tour minibus raced on through the English countryside heading south. And the further south they went the harder it rained. At last they reached the coast. The road turned to the west so on one side of the tour minibus were rolling hills covered with specks of white sheep and on the other side was a stormy, frothing, foamy sea covered in white horses.

A jolt woke Cressida. The rest of the Daisy Drama Club were still fast asleep including Pickle and Wolfgang. The twins Harry and Hen looked like a pile of spaghetti, long arms wrapped around each other, plaits of red hair all jumbled up and freckles on their noses like a sprinkling of cheese just to finish off. Next to them Susie was sitting by Beaky. Susie was cuddling her fluffy lamb that was just as fluffy as

Susie's hair which kept tickling Beaky's nose, making Beaky twitch. Beaky had a long, sharp nose which was why she was called Beaky - but she was proud of her nose because Grandpa Albert had a long nose too. Abby, Lou and Alice were sitting on the other side. Abby had a book called *Ten Top Tips to Control Your Pony* on her lap which was just about to fall onto the floor. Lou had been sewing beads onto a costume and had the sewing box just by her foot which she was in danger of kicking over. Alice had her head pushed against the window, a pencil for her sketching wobbling in her hand and Wolfgang was leaning on her, snuffling and snorting and dreaming of chasing big, fat, fluffy rabbits.

Cressida had a big file called *DDC ON TOUR FILE* and opened it at *Tour Timetable*. The *Tour Timetable* was one of the most important pieces of paper of the whole tour. The DDC were performing *The Lighthouseman and the Monster of the Deep* three times. It would be important to make the most of the bits of time between shows.

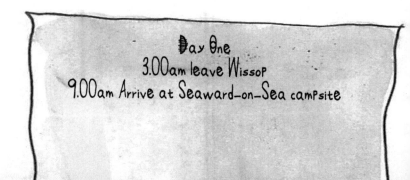

Day One
3.00am leave Wissop
9.00am Arrive at Seaward-on-Sea campsite

11.00am Put up tents
2.00pm Performance 1 at *Lady of the Waves Theatre*

Day Two
10.00am Rehearse mistakes made yesterday
11.00am Morning on beach having fun
2.00pm Performance 2 at *The Cave Theatre*

Day Three
10.00am Rehearse mistakes made yesterday
11.00am Morning on beach having fun
2.00pm Performance 3 at *The Turnaround Theatre*
5.00pm Home to Wissop
The END

Sophie was leaning on Cressida's shoulder, her mouth wide open, snoring. Her head was jabbing Cressie's shoulder. Cressie slowly tried to move position without waking her best friend. But another jolt and Sophie woke up.

'Are we there?' she asked sitting up.

'Not yet,' replied Cressida in a whisper. 'But we must be getting close. Look.'

Sophie rubbed the steam off the window and peered outside. They were driving along a cliff road. A long way below Sophie could see the sea crashing onto the black jagged rocks and as she looked further out she saw great rolling waves on a stormy sea.

'The sea!' cried Sophie. 'I can see the sea!'

'Shh,' said Cressie. 'Everyone else is asleep and we've got lots to do.'

But it was too late. Everyone was waking up.

'The sea! I can see the sea!' echoed around the minibus.

'Tho can I thort of, but it'th all tho thteamed up!'

Heavy rain sloshed down from black clouds. The wipers, which squeaked backwards and forwards, tried to keep the windscreen clear but it was almost impossible.

'Where are we?' asked Uncle Max leaning forward and trying his hardest to see out.

'Just keep going!' said John trying to make head or tail of the map and giving up. He looked up and in the distance saw a light flashing on ... off ... on ...off. 'Look! We must be nearly there. Seaward-on-Sea Lighthouse!'

'Head for the lighthouse!' cried Millie. 'With all this water I almost feel that I am in a boat! Oh what an adventure! Isn't this thrilling!'

Uncle Max drove along a cliff edge then down a steep hill and past a sign that said *Welcome to Seaward-on-Sea - where every day is a holiday!* Attached to the sign but blowing around so hard that nobody could read it was another sign saying *FESTIVAL.* On they drove down into the little village, splashing past whitewashed houses, stone houses, a butcher's, a baker's, a candlestick maker's and down, down to the harbour where fishing boats were tossing up and down on the choppy water, past a beach with the sand and sea one side of the road and a wooden beach hut cafe on the other. The road narrowed but still it went on towards the lighthouse.

Still the lighthouse light flashed on, off, on, off!

'Nearly there,' cried Millie again. 'Oh, what an adventure! I can't wait to send my dear creaky old people a postcard.'

At last Uncle Max pulled up at the edge of the water. Ahead stretched out the causeway, the rocky road laid over rocks. At the far end of the road was the lighthouse. But each time a wave rolled in the road was covered in spray and swirling, whirling seawater.

'That,' said Uncle Max, 'is a challenge.'

'You're not going to try and drive acroth are you?' came an anxious voice from the back. 'I really am not a very good thwimmer!'

'Of course not!' said Millie answering for Uncle Max. 'I don't think we need to. Look!'

Lighthouse Breakfast

Through the swirling waters they could just make out a boat heading towards them. It was a small tug boat with a tiny cabin but what was so strange was that nobody seemed to be steering it. The boat rolled and pitched and pitched and rolled in the frothy waves. As it came towards land, at the last moment, just before crashing into a barnacled old wooden jetty, the tub boat swerved violently to starboard (that is the *right*) and a rope was hurled into the air.

A small figure, so small that he had not been spotted in the tug boat, leapt ashore and tied the boat with astonishing speed to a ring on the jetty.

The figure marched up to Uncle Max's window and tapped on the glass. A high pitched voice squeaked, 'Welcome to Seaward-on-Sea!'

Uncle Max wound down the window.

The most tiddly sized sea captain you could ever imagine, wearing a sea captain's hat, head to toe oilskins and a very large, bright orange life jacket, was grinning up at him.

'I am Captain Turnaround Junior,' he said. 'The Captain, that is my father Captain Turnaround the lighthouse man, sent me to pick you up in our tug boat *Loosey Goosey* which we normally use for towing boats that have got stuck *on* the rocks *off* the rocks but today I have come to pick you up because the weather is so ferociously fearsome and the Captain, that's my dad of course, but we all call him Captain, is busy working the lantern to show you the way so he couldn't come across himself and we'll have to go in

Loosey Goosey because we still haven't found the secret underground tunnel that takes you from the lighthouse to land or from land to the lighthouse but we don't know where it is because when the pirates came hundreds of years ago the lighthouse man, my lots of greats grandfather ago, only left us a code which we need to crack to tell us the riddle which we need to solve which tells you where the secret tunnel is but we can't crack the code so we can't solve the riddle so we have to come across in *Loosey Goosey* but sometimes we can't because the sea is too rough and we have to stay in the lighthouse for weeks and weeks and eat dried fish from our store.'

This was a long speech but already John had picked up that there could be more to this holiday than just doing the lighting! And so had Millie.

'Oh I say!' she cried. 'How very, very exciting. I will have to tell my creaky old people but how I will fit all this thrilling news on one postcard I do not know!'

The DDC put on all the waterproofs they could find and clambered aboard *Loosey Goosey* with Pickle and Wolfgang. Captain Turnaround Junior cast off the *Loosey Goosey* and headed out into the churning waters.

It was not a long journey but poor Susie was terrified and started to feel sick. She hung onto the side of *Loosey Goosey* for dear life. But worse was to come. As the boat reached another little jetty by the rocky island Captain Turnaround Junior gave orders.

'When the wave pushes us up you jump down!' he yelled above the sound of the crashing waters. 'Don't worry if you fall. Mrs Turnaround will catch you!'

Susie, who was desperate to get off the boat, surprised everyone by making a leap for dry land. Her successful landing gave everyone courage and one by one the rest of the DDC, John, Millie, Uncle Max, Wolfgang and Pickle jumped ashore.

'Welcome! Welcome!' came a jolly voice as they each hurled themselves into the outstretched arms of Mrs Turnaround who was waiting on the jetty. But the words of the jolly voice were snatched away by the wind and half buried by the speaker's souwester making it very hard to hear.

'I am Mrs Turnaround, the lady of the lighthouse. Steady! Oh this wind and rain! Take care! At least it's not a hurricane! Mind your step! Sometimes we are trapped in the lighthouse for weeks on end when we can't even get to shore on *Loosey Goosey* and we still haven't solved the riddle of the secret tunnel the lots of great grandfathers ago left us! Down you come! The weather was so bad earlier that poor, dearest Captain Turnaround had to get up in the middle of the night to put on the emergency light. Oh a wolfhound! How lovely! And a pony! Better still! Come in! Come in!'

The DDC hurried into the lighthouse out of the stormy weather. Inside was a kitchen which looked just like a kitchen except all the walls were curved and the table was a circle which fitted perfectly into the room and in middle of the table was another circle cut out so more children could sit in the middle of the table. Sitting round the table and *in* the table were twelve children all wearing thickly knitted navy blue jumpers.

They were tremendously excited when they saw Pickle and jumped up to rub him down and warm him up.

'What's its name?'

'Is it boy or a girl?'

'How old is it?'

'Can it swim?'

'Has it ever been to a lighthouse before?'

'Does it eat fish?'

'Breakfast children!' commanded Mrs Turnaround. 'Very well you may have your breakfast on board the pony if you insist,' she added to the youngest three who had already clambered onto Pickle's back.

Turning to the DDC she introduced her children.

'This is Captain Turnaround Junior, or Tom who brought you over in *Loosey Goosey*, and Tim, Trixie, Truffle, Teddy, Trumpet, Triangle, Trapdoor and Truck and Toffee, Tadpole and Trousers on your pony. The Captain and I loved names beginning with T but we soon ran out of them so we just used the names of the first thing we saw beginning with T after the baby was born. So Trousers was named after Truffle's trousers which were on the line and Tadpole was named after Triangle's tadpole and Trixie left a toffee stuck to the door handle so that is Toffee and Truck was Triangle's Christmas present and Triangle was because Tim joined percussion and Trumpet was because Trixie joined brass, Teddy was Tom's teddy

72

and Truffle was what I bought dearest Captain Turnaround for his birthday and Trapdoor is - oh here is Captain Turnaround!'

As Mrs Turnaround spoke there was a banging sound from above. A trapdoor opened in the ceiling, a rope ladder flew down and a very thin man with a long beard and pointy nose shot down onto the breakfast table.

'The Daisy Drama Club themselves!' he said in a booming voice that sounded much too big for his body. 'What an honour! What an honour! Dreadful weather! Dreadful weather! I've been up at the top, up at the top making sure the light was turning, turning to welcome you in. Welcome! Welcome! Now tuck in! Tuck in!'

Captain Turnaround leapt like a goat off the table and took his place in the middle of the table between Triangle and Truck.

'I'll say it again because I say everything again, tuck in! Tuck in! It comes with living in a lighthouse for so long and everything going round and round in circles. Circles!'

The Daisy Drama Club, John, Uncle Max and Millie squeezed themselves in amongst the Turnaround children. It was the strangest looking breakfast they had every seen. Fish, fish and more fish! Mrs Turnaround saw their faces.

'Don't you worry if you don't fancy fish at this time of day! Lots of our campers don't. It's just what *we* eat! We have cereal for *landies.*'

'*Landies* are what we call people who don't live in lighthouses,' said Triangle.

'Which of you *landies* would like cereal?'

The DDC all shot up their hands.

'I thought so,' said Mrs Turnaround smiling. She opened a cupboard and had a look.

'Now let me see. We've got brown shrimp flakes, limpet pops, sea beet bix or clam bran. What would you like dear?'

The question was directed at Susie who could hardly speak in horror.

Cressida, meanwhile, was not thinking about cereal. Two things were puzzling her. Firstly, she had noticed that Captain Turnaround and the Turnaround children looked somehow familiar. She could not say exactly *why* but there was *something* about them. Secondly, there were some very strange characters written on the walls round the kitchen ...

... not high but low and in you go
... at the end of the Flow peep low
... not bottom but top and out you pop ...

'That's the code,' said Tom seeing Cressida look puzzled.

'But we can't crack it,' said Tim.

'So we can't solve the riddle,' added Trixie.

'Although we've tried ...' added Truffle.

'... and tried ...' added Teddy.

'... and tried ...' added Trumpet.

'... and tried ...' added Triangle.

'... and tried ...' added Trapdoor.

'... and tried ...' added Truck.

'... and given up,' sighed Toffee, Tadpole and Trousers.

'If we could crack the code we could solve the riddle and find the secret passage our lots of greats grandfather ago hid from the pirates. The pirates,' explained Captain Turnaround.

'And then we wouldn't be marooned here when the bad weather sets in,' added Mrs Turnaround.

Cressida and Sophie looked at each other knowing exactly what each other was thinking just as best friends do. A code was something that needed cracking and a riddle was something that needed solving and if they could help the Turnarounds find the secret passage they jolly well would!

Breakfast over, Captain Turnaround announced it was time to put up tents. Put up tents.

The DDC looked out of the small round windows to see if it was still raining. Putting up tents in the rain was tricky.

'No rain! No rain!' said the lighthouse man. ' All bright as a button now! A button!'

It was true.

When the DDC went outside the torrential rain had stopped, the angry black clouds had blown away, and the sun was out, glinting and glittering on the calm sea. Waves no longer crashed over the causeway so Uncle Max was able to drive the tour minibus right across to the campsite.

Tom, Tim, Trixie, Truffle, Teddy, Trumpet, Triangle, Trapdoor, Truck, Toffee, Tadpole and Trousers helped the Daisy Drama Club get out the tents and started to put them up on the lighthouse campsite. This was a little area besides the lighthouse and surrounded by a white washed stone wall, so it was beautifully sheltered from howling winds.

'We can tie Pickle to Pirate's Ear Ring,' said Toffee threading the rope from Pickle's halter through an iron ring attached to the wall and tying an incredible knot at incredible speed.

Tying knots of all sorts was part of the Turnaround children's education.

'It's the ring they used to tie pirates to,' added Tadpole.

'Until the pirates rotted away,' finished Trousers.

Abby wasn't sure if Pickle would like being tied to Pirate's Ear Ring but Pickle was munching away at some particularly juicy looking grass so she just hoped he had not heard what Toffee, Tadpole and Trousers had said. She did not want Pickle having nightmares.

Meanwhile the DDC and the rest of the Turnarounds were discovering that pitching tents even in a shelterered spot is not easy.

Uncle Max had borrowed five ridge tents from the Wissop scouts and the DDC and young Turnarounds soon had canvas flapping wildly in their faces, poles falling over in all directions and lots of knotty problems on their hands.

Millie clapped her hands and giggled. 'Oh dear,' she cried. 'Let me help. Now let me see.'

Millie had spent her childhood in the girl guides and her girl guide shirt was covered in the thirty five badges she had earned including *Survival*, *Outdoor Cook*, *First Aid*, *Camper* and *Camper Advanced* badges so she knew exactly what to do. First Millie got all the groundsheets laid out in a nice semi-circle pattern and asked the Turnaround children to kindly sit on them so the groundsheets didn't blow away. Then she asked the DDC to peg the groundsheets firmly into the ground. Then with ridge poles assembled, upright poles slotted together, spikes fed into eyelets and dollies attached to storm guys the tents were raised and main guy lines tightened. The camp was pitched.

Seconds later Millie had even got a kettle merrily boiling on a little campfire. Uncle Max was impressed. What a wife!

'Now,' said Millie beaming round at everyone. 'Who would like a cup of cocoa?'

Millie sends Postcard No 1

My Dear Creaky Old People,

I am sitting peeping out of my tent at the beautiful blue of the English sea. This is a picture of Seaward-on-Sea Lighthouse. Seaward-on-Sea is such a pretty, pretty place. I do so wish you were here. We could paddle in the sea and collect lots of shells for our nature table at Bluebell House. Hope you are keeping warm and eating healthily and not forgetting to go out for a nice walk each day and if you do don't forget to put on your ... here Mille ran out of room so she finished quickly ... Lots of love and hugs and kisses Millie xxxxx

SEAWARD-ON-SEA LIGHT HOUSE

WHERE EVERY DAY IS A HOLIDAY

The Festival is Open!

While they were enjoying their cocoa Captain Turnaround bounced into the campsite waving a *Programme of Events.* The *Programme of Events* said ...

SEAWARD-on-SEA FESTIVAL
Programme of Events

DAY ONE
Grand Opening *by* Trumpet
2.00pm FIRST PERFORMANCE - DDC
Lady of the Waves Theatre

DAY TWO
2.00pm SECOND PERFORMANCE - DDC
The Cave Theatre, Castaway Bay

DAY THREE
2.00pm THIRD PERFORMANCE - DDC
The Turnaround Theatre
Closing Ceremony *by* Trumpet

SPECIAL NOTE
Audiences - *please meet by the flagpole*
on the causeway for all performances

✿ 81 ✿

'Why does the audience need to meet by the flagpole for all the performances if the performances are in different places?' asked Lou.

'They *are* in different places,' agreed Captain Turnaround. 'But they start in the *same* place! The *same* place! And you, as performers need to be at the flagpole earlier so you are ready for curtain up! Curtain up!'

Sophie and Cressida looked at each other and exchanged anxious glances. They had expected to go to a different theatre each day, not stand by a flagpole. They had imagined going *on tour* would involve moving from one place to another, not standing still.

'Are there any other performers coming?' asked Abby looking at the list.

'Oh no! No!' said Captain Turnaround. 'No-one else could come or *would* come so we were extra pleased when you said you *could* and *would*! Extra pleased! Otherwise it would not have been a very good festival at all. Not at all!'

No more questions could be asked because Captain Turnaround was shouting out orders to his children. 'Tom and Tim, bunting up! Trixie, Truffle, and Teddy, make sure the splendid posters Alice has brought are on every lamppost, noticeboard, shop window and everywhere else. Trumpet and Triangle, you are in charge of visitor parking so make sure everyone parks out in Faraway Fields then bring them round by boat if they don't want to walk over the clifftop. Trapdoor and Truck, you are in charge of performers, that is the Daisy Drama Club, so make sure they know where they are meant to be and what they are meant to be doing and that they are not hungry or lost. Toffee, Tadpole and Trousers, you are on ticket sales so make sure every performance is a sensational super sellout!'

'Could we use Pickle as our Box Office?' asked Toffee.

'We could ride him all over Seaward-on-Sea selling tickets,' added Tadpole.

'Please,' added Trousers.

Pickle neighed in approval, so that was that.

'Everybody clear? Quite clear!' concluded Captain Turnaround. 'Three days of theatrical fun starts now! Right now!'

'Shall I sound the opening of the festival Captain?' asked Trumpet who was in charge of loud noises.

'By Neptune's barnacles! Yes! We have only

twenty-three seconds to go! Stations everyone! Everyone!'

Instead of blowing a trumpet as the DDC expected, Trumpet climbed up onto the walls surrounding the lighthouse and lit the big black iron cannon that pointed menacingly out to sea.

There was a terrific boom! Bang! Boom! Boom!

Out of the cannon shot a banner that flew over the bay. On the banner was written in red letters ...

'Seaward-on-Sea Festival open! Open!'

In a flash all the little Turnarounds, except for Trapdoor and Truck, had disappeared.

'We will meet you at the flagpole at half past twelve,' said Trapdoor to the DDC.

'Make sure you have everything you need like costumes ...' added Truck.

'... and props ...' added Trapdoor.

'... and other things ...' added Truck not sure what other things you would need for a play.

And off they shot, carrying fishing rods, down the causeway at top speed, overtaking Toffee, Tadpole and Trousers who had trotted off on Pickle and were waving a big sign saying *Box Office*.

Millie sends Postcard No 2

My Dear Creaky Old People,

I just had to write and tell you that the festival is now open! Dear Sir Hugh, you would have been so thrilled. Trumpet fired a cannon! The noise was deafening. I'm surprised you didn't hear it in Wissop. And there is a code that needs cracking and a riddle that needs solving but ... here Mille ran out of room so she quickly finished ... Lots of love and hugs and kisses Millie xxxxx

A Watery Performance

At one o'clock the Daisy Drama Club and John were standing by the flagpole near the jetty waiting for they were not sure what. Trapdoor and Truck turned up with a picnic lunch of fish, fish and more fish, freshly caught. Luckily Millie had put together a little hamper just as tasty.

'The *Lady of the Waves Theatre* will be here soon,' said Trapdoor.

Beaky tapped her nose anxiously.

'That sounds odd. Surely *we* should be going to the theatre, not the theatre coming to *us*.'

'Wait and see! Wait and see!' said Truck.

'Here she is!' cried Trapdoor.

And there she was, bobbing along on the *sea*!

They knew she was the theatre because there was a big sign saying *Lady of the Waves Theatre*.

The DDC stared in amazement. Normally a theatre would have at least solid brick walls and a door and a roof. Perhaps even a window or two and steps to go up to go inside. And you would know there would be rows and rows of seats and a stage with a curtain and a backstage and a green room and maybe even dressing rooms. This theatre did not look as if it would have hardly any of these things.

'It's a fishing boat!' cried Abby.

'How can we perform a play on a fishing boat?' added Lou. 'We'll be bouncing around all the time!'

'And where will the audience sit?' added Alice.

Sophie and Cressida were speechless with shock! Upset! Bursting with disappointment! They had dreamt of performing in a *real* theatre. Not a *fishing boat!* It wasn't even a particularly big fishing boat so it would make a very, very little theatre.

Captain Turnaround came out of the lighthouse and ran down the causeway to the flagpole.

'Welcome to the *Lady of the Waves Theatre*. Welcome! A beauty isn't she? Isn't she?'

'Thee'th very fithy!' sniffed Susie as the fishing boat drew alongside the jetty.

'What do you expect?' bellowed a deep voice from the guts of the boat. There was the sound of heavy footsteps climbing upwards and a fisherman with the most enormous white beard dappled with fish scales and fish bones and dressed in a bright yellow oilskin fishing smock, waterproof waders and wellies

 88

emerged, threw a rope to Captain Turnaround and the two of them moored up the *Lady of the Waves Theatre*. 'We've been out since before sunrise this morning,' went on the fisherman in a very deep, very slow voice, 'catching, let me see now ... oh yes ... bass ... and cod ... and mullet ... and tope ... and turbot ... and flounder ... and ling, so of course *Lady of the Waves* is a bit fishy! Be odd if she wasn't. She is a fishing boat after all.'

'Except when she's being a theatre,' added Captain Turnaround. 'A theatre!'

'Oh how lovely!' said Millie, who had been crabbing with Uncle Max. 'Are we going on a fishing trip. I *love* fishing!'

'No,' said Abby gloomily. 'This is the theatre.'

'Oh no it's not! No it's not!' said Captain Turnaround. 'There you are quite wrong. Wrong! It's not *the* theatre. It's the *first* theatre of the festival. Trapdoor and Truck, show the DDC aboard. Green room! Backstage! Wings! Dressing rooms! Stage! All aboard! All aboard!'

The fisherman lumbered off muttering about landies having 'No idea! no idea!' and passed Toffee, Tadpole and Trousers who were trotting down the causeway on Pickle towards the fishing boat.

'Captain! Captain! Captain!' shouted Toffee, Tadpole and Trousers.

'We've sold *all* the *Lady of the Waves* tickets.'

'It's a sellout!'

'By turbot! Good work! Good work! Go and buy yourselves ice-creams! Ice-creams!'

'And *we* had better get aboard,' added Cressida,

trying her best to hide her disappointment about the theatre. 'We need to be ready for the audience.'

'The audienth!' said Susie, suddenly alarmed.

The *audience*!

For the first time Susie suddenly realised she did not *know* the audience. All their other plays had been performed in The Barn Theatre and the audience had been made up of the DDC's mums and dads and uncles and aunts and grandpas and grandmas and friends and a few friends of friends. Now they were going to perform to perfect strangers! Unknowns! The general public! What if the audience didn't like the play? What if they booed! Or threw bad eggs or bits of fish at them? Or just walked off?

'Susie, are you feeling seasick already?' asked Cressida. Susie looked pale in a greenish sort of way.

'It's just the audienth. We don't *know* them. They might not *like* uth!'

'Susie,' snapped Sophie, still upset, 'that is all part of the *excitement* of going on tour. We have to face the unexpected! The unknown!'

As she said it she realised that was *exactly* what they had to do - *face the unexpected*. She grinned at Cressie who grinned back, both thinking the same as best friends do. They would make the most of the *Lady of the Waves Theatre* whatever it took!

'And don't forget, Susie, we are the Daisy Drama Club,' added Cressida. 'We will put on a really good show *wherever* we are ... even if it's on a fishing boat!'

Trapdoor led the way into the pilot house, which was the little hut-like cabin on deck, then disappeared down a short stepladder to below decks. The DDC followed. Below decks was small, cramped, dark and stank of fish. On a tiny door on the starboard side was a sign saying *dressing room* which led to a tiny cabin. On a tiny door on the port side was a sign which said *make-up* which led to an even tinier cabin.

'The rest of the space is your backstage, wings and green room. The stage is on deck. Break a leg!'

And with that Trapdoor had gone up the stepladder and disappeared.

'It thtinkth of fith!' said Susie holding her nose and completely forgetting how worried she had been about the audience now she was nearly passing out from the stink of fish.

'Leaping liquorice. It's pitch black!' said Harry.

'Leaping liquorice. I can't see a thing,' added Hen.

'Do you need some lights down there?' came a voice from above.

It was John. His lights would be wasted on deck in broad daylight so they might as well be used to light up below decks. Soon the cabins were flooded with light from the red and green spotlights.

'We better get ready super speedily,' said Sophie, 'and then everyone have a peep at the stage.'

'Oh yeth,' said Susie. 'We mutht know all our entranceth and exitth otherwith we might end up in the thea!'

As soon as Sophie and Cressida were in costume and made up they poked their heads on deck. To their amazement a swarm of Turnaround children, with the help of Uncle Max, Millie and John, had transformed the fishing boat into a tiny theatre.

A stage had been constructed: short driftwood planks were laid inside the pilot house, balancing on old lobster pots; three long driftwood planks were balanced outside the pilot house from the port gunwale to the starboard gunwale which are the rails on top of the hull which is the part of the ship from the very bottom up to the top where it meets the deck. Next Uncle Max, Mille and John, with the help of Trapdoor and Truck, had brought aboard the scenery and props and set them out exactly in the positions they had planned at home in The Barn Theatre.

In the centre of the stage was the rocky island.

 93

On the island was Angelica's invention box. On the edge of the island was Cornet's fishing rod and bucket, ready for action. The only difference from The Barn Theatre was the size of the stage. It was teeny weeny.

More driftwood planks had been laid out on the deck, balancing on more lobster pots, ready for the audience to sit on. Toffee was standing behind a little table made of driftwood balanced on yet another lobster pot, which had a sign saying *Tickets* and another sign saying *Programmes* and another sign saying *Toffees*.

Tadpole and Trousers were riding Pickle up and down the causeway handing out lifejackets to the audience, who were waiting in a long line from the flagpole, and checking everyone had tickets before they embarked and before Toffee checked their tickets again.

'Are you ready?' shouted Tadpole.

'Ready!' shouted back Trapdoor.

Sophie and Cressida looked at each other in surprise. Were *they* ready? But ready or not the audience started to embark.

Sophie and Cressida were determined that the DDC would give the audience the best show they had ever seen. With their hearts thumping with that excited feeling they always got just before the start of a performance, they hurried down the ladder to the below decks backstage to tell the rest of the cast that the world premiere performance of *The Lighthouse Man and the Monster Eel* was about to begin!

But below decks all was *not* ready.

Lou was still hard at work on the make-up. The boat was gentle rocking in a rather sick making way and the light was red and green in a rather sick looking way. And to make matters worse Susie, as official assistant, kept offering to help Lou and she really, in Lou's opinion, was NOT THAT HELPFUL. Lou had her DDC make-up book so she knew *exactly* what to do *on her own*. She just had Beaky and Alice left to do.

But Susie was not easily put off.

'Shall I make up Alith for you Lou?'

'No! I'm fine Susie! Just fine!' said Lou. Susie could be *so* annoying sometimes.

'Are you thure? I am your athithtant here to help. It would be no trouble and curtain up will be thoon!'

'No! I'm sure I'm sure Susie.'

There was really not enough room for one

96

make-up artist let alone two below decks.

Lou worked as fast as she could on Beaky.

'Finished!' she said at last putting the final touches to Beaky's make-up. Beaky took a look in Lou's DDC make-up department mirror which Lou did allow Susie to hold.

'That's wonderful Lou ... but I look like Maximus the Monster Eel,' said Beaky.

'But you *are* Maximus the Monster Eel!'

'No. *I'm* Lachlan the Lighthouse Man! *Alice* is Maximus!'

Lou went white with shock.

'Ready?' called down John. 'The audience is all aboard. Beginners in position ready for curtain up!'

'Aaaah!' screamed Lou. 'That's me! Wait! Oh help! What shall I do?'

'Don't worry Lou,' said Susie calmly. 'You're thuch

a good teacher - I know exactly what to do! Quick. Let's wath off Beaky's fath, put on thome emergenthy lighthouth man stripeth. That'th perfect. You two go and get on thtage and I'll paint the monthter eel on Alith. It'th all under control Lou. Don't forget the DDC ith a team!'

'Oh thank you! I'm sorry Susie! Thank you!'

A sudden most enormous bang made them all jump. Trumpet had fired another cannon. On deck Captain Turnaround was making a speech.

'Ladies and Gentlemen, fishermen, friends and friendly fishermen. Friendly fishermen. Welcome to the Seaward-on-Sea Festival. Welcome. The fantasticalicas Daisy Drama Club will now perform the world premiere of *The Lighthouse Man and the Monster Eel*. Oh! Such a monster eel!'

Captain Turnaround sat down on the front row next to Mrs Turnaround. John drew back a curtain, that had been put up by Trumpet and Trousers, to reveal the rocky island. Cornet was fishing, Angelica was inventing and Beaky, the lighthouse man, was turning and turning and turning.

From the cabin emerged Lou as Merman. Her heart was pounding. How could she have made such a stupid mistake? She climbed the stepladder up into the pilot house which formed the back of the stage and just as she was about to start she heard a little voice far down below saying, 'That'th perfect Alith. You look thooper thcarey.'

Lou breathed a huge sigh of relief. If Susie could rise to the occasion so could she. In her most mermany, mysterious, underwatery way, Lou began the play.

```
MERMAN
    Come, take my hand
    And together we'll slip
    Beneath the breaking waves,
    Under the swaying waters of endless blue.
    We'll leap with the dolphins,
    Snatch a flash of silver fish
    And rejoice in the song
    Of the humpbacked whales.
    But onwards and deeper down we'll go,
    To a green frond world
    Of waving weed and barnacled wrecks.
    Of wistful mermaids
    And black-eyed monsters cold.
    Deep, deep down we'll slowly swim
    To the shadowy, mysterious, magical waters
    Of oceans deep.
```

The Lighthouse Man and the Monster Eel had begun!

All At Sea!

The performance went according to plan until scene two when disaster struck ...

Alice climbed up the stepladder and slithered and wriggled onto the stage as Maximus the Monster Eel. She had just begun to speak in her evil, monstrously monster of the deep sort of way ...

```
I am the monstrous monster of the deep.
A giant eel with black, unblinking eye.
Slowly and menacingly I glide - WHOA!
```

... when she nearly fell over.

The fishing boat was MOVING!

'Sorry folks one and all!' said the very deep, very slow voice of the fisherman who had been on board earlier. 'I have just got to check my lobster pots.'

The fisherman, who now also had biscuit crumbs and dribbles of coffee dribbling off his beard, as well as fish scales and fish bones, had squeezed his way on board, through the audience, into the pilot house and *started up the engine*!

It was now a tight squeeze in the pilot house, with actors and fishermen trying to do quite different jobs.

The fishing boat trembled, gurgled and lurched forward. The *Lady of the Waves Theatre* was on the move! What could Alice do? ...

... there was nothing for it but to carry on!

```
Slowly and menacingly I glide,
In and out of the waving weeds, where I hide
Lurking - ready to leap and snatch my prey.
So beware! Take care!
One day, my prey
To chomp and chew and spit and spew might be ...
          ... YOU!
```

The *Lady of the Waves Theatre* chugged out of the harbour and onto the open seas. It was now a fine day but out at sea it was choppy and salty water sprayed over the audience as the boat ploughed on.

All went well until Alice came on stage disguised as the ice-cream seller.

```
MAXIMUS (disguised as ice-cream seller)
   This is a cunning disguise.
   I'll give this fisher boy a nasty surprise!
   Ha! Ha! Ha! Ha!
   Ice-creams! Delicious ice-creams! Ice-creams!

CORNET
   Ice-creams! My favourite!

MAXIMUS
   What will you have, young man?
   Stickleback cornetto or frozen walrus whip?
   Vanilla cornet with dead fin dip?
```

Mouldy oyster with barracuda chip?
Baked bear ice-bar? - that's hip
Pincer tub with sharkfin topping?
- careful of the nip -
Or turtle soup lolly with shrimp jelly?
- very jolly ...

'I'd like a vanilla cornet with dead fin dip,' came a voice from the audience.

'Could I have four pincer tubs with sharkfin topping,' added a chubby dad with three chubby children.

'That turtle soup lolly sounds jolly nice,' said a thin lady whose hair was being blown about so much it looked as if it might come off.

Alice was confused. What a silly audience! Didn't they realise that the ice-creams were *pretend*?

'I think *I* can oblige,' said the fisherman. 'Open that freezer box you're standing on young man,' he said to John, 'and you should find ice-creams. We always go *out* to sea with the freezer box full of ice-creams and come *back* with the freezer box full of fish. Lucky for you we're going out.'

John opened the lid and there were boxes and boxes of choc ices.

'Hand them out,' went on the fisherman generously. 'You're all welcome! All welcome!'

The audience licked their ice-creams, the play continued and the *Lady of the Waves Theatre* headed further out to sea.

At the very moment Lachlan the Lighthouse Man discovers his children are missing the *Lady of the Waves Theatre* reached the lobster pots. The fisherman stopped the engine to check the pots. The sudden silence and the sadness of the lighthouse man who had lost his children moved many of the audience to tears.

```
LACHLAN THE LIGHTHOUSE MAN
    Bloomin' barnacles!
    Every time I turn my back
    Another child disappears!
    Bloomin' barnacles I'm all alone ...
            ... alone
                    ... ALONE!
    It's all my fault.
    I've been dedicated to sea and salt.
    What a bad dad I am -
    A bad, bad dad.
    Hopeless! Neglectful!
    Selfish! A fool!
```

```
I've got to keep turning to keep earning
And to save great ships from starting to sink
Yet I've let my own children
Perish in the brink.
My minds all awhirl.
I've lost my boy and my girl.
Strange sailors I've strived to save
But abandoned by own children
To a watery grave.
Angelica!
Cornet!
Wherever you are
Don't give up on your bad old dad!
I can't stop turning but ... ooooh!
I'm getting a pain.
My heart is bursting to see you again!
```

It was a long speech and Beaky was magnificent. Sobs came from the audience and the chubby dad cuddled his three chubby children closer.

The fisherman hauled in a lobster pot with one large surprised looking lobster and started up the engine again. With a chug, chug, chug, the fishing boat set off back for shore.

At the same time the play continued. Even the lobster seemed to enjoy the show, waving it's antennae at Susie, the pretty Princess Crabella.

The final bow came just as the *Lady of the Waves Theatre* drew alongside the jetty. The audience clapped and cheered. Not only had they enjoyed the play but they had had a splendid ride out to sea.

Sophie and Cressida grinned at each other, knowing what each other was thinking as only best friends do. The first performance of the Daisy Drama Club tour had been a sensational success in a super surprising way!

What was even more surprising was that Captain Turnaround, who had been transfixed by the play, had leapt ashore as soon as the *Lady of the Waves Theatre* had reached land and had dashed into his lighthouse without saying a word.

The weather was fine, not a cloud in the sky.

There was no need to warn sailors of storms.

What could he be up to?

Millie sends Postcard No 3

My Dear Creaky Old People,
What a lovely performance. Out at sea! The real
lobster was such a dear! Hope you are keeping warm
and eating healthily and not forgetting to go out for
a nice walk each day and if you do don't forget to
put on your ... here Mille ran out of room and so she
finished quickly ... Lots of love and hugs and kisses
Millie xxxxx

SEAWARD-ON-SEA

SEAWARD-ON-SEA BEACH SHOP

ICE
CREAMS

WHERE EVERY DAY IS A HOLIDAY

Captain Turnaround's Discovery

Captain Turnaround climbed the rope ladder that dangled down from the kitchen ceiling, flung open the trapdoor and raced up the twirly whirly helter-skelter stairs four at a time to get to the very top room of the lighthouse. They were called the helter-skelter stairs because you went *up* the stairs round and round, but to save time there was a slide to come *down*, just like a helter-skelter.

In the very top room, set into the wall, was a secret little door. It was secret because it had no handle and you wouldn't spot it unless you were eagle-eyed. But Captain Turnaround knew it was there. He went straight to it and pressed. The door sprang open to reveal a hole cut away into the wall of the lighthouse itself. And in this hole was a massive, ancient, dusty book. On the front of the book written in dark, blood red letters were the words ...

The Complete
and Total
History
of Seaward-on-Sea
Lighthouse

Captain Turnaround blew off the dust. He opened the cover and thumbed through the pages. He went backwards through the book until he came to a drawing of the very first owner.

'By Neptune's knuckles! I'm right!'

Captain Turnaround had been reading *The Complete and Total History of Seaward-on-Sea Lighthouse* for many years. Each chapter was about each Seaward-on-Sea lighthouse man and each lighthouse man was the son of the lighthouse man before him.

So Captain Turnaround had been most interested to read about his own father, then his grandfather, then his great grandfather so he had decided to read the book starting from *The End* and was still a long way off from reaching *The Beginning* and *Chapter One* which would be about the very first lighthouse man his very, very many grandfathers ago. Now having flicked hundreds of pages backwards he found himself looking at a faded drawing of the first lighthouse man of Seaward-on-Sea Lighthouse.

'Aha!' Just as Captain Turnaround suspected.

The very first lighthouse man distinctly had a light on his head. *The DDC play must be about the very first lighthouse man of Seaward-on-Sea Lighthouse!*

Captain Turnaround kicked his heels in the air!

Underneath the picture was a caption.

CAPTAIN L 'Tunneller' TURNAROUND - KNOWN AS *TUNNELLER* FOR THE SECRET ESCAPE TUNNEL HE DUG TO SAVE HIS SON AND DAUGHTER ANGELICA AND CORNET, FROM UNWELCOME PIRATES, AFTER A NASTY EPISODE WITH THE GRUESOME PIRATE GRUNGRAG AND THE CREW OF BLACK BONES

Captain Turnaround read Chapter One from end to beginning. There were many mentions of eels, especially one monster one that became quite tame and lived in the rock pool by the jetty.

There was also a thrilling paragraph about the nasty episode with Pirate Grungrag which would make a lovely hammocktime story to tell the little Turnarounds when they were all snuggled up, gently rocking to sleep in their hammocks.

How thoughtful, thought the Captain, of the DDC to perform a play about the first Seaward-on-Sea lighthouse man. But how did they know the story? Hadn't one of them written the play? Wasn't it the girl who always had her nose in a book just like his sister Ethel. Yes! Beaky! What a name! And what a nose! And wasn't it a nose just like Ethel's nose ... *and* the noses of all the little Turnarounds. And as for that his own nose. Beaky noses ran in his family. Well nose or no nose, it was very clever of Beaky to have written about the first lighthouse man of Seaward-on-Sea. And how clever *he* was to have worked it out!

Captain Turnaround put the ancient, dusty book back and closed the secret little door. He slid down the helter-skelter, through the trapdoor, down the rope ladder into the kitchen and out into the fresh air, kicking his heels together again in delight.

First Night under the Stars

Round the campfire that evening the DDC sang two sea shanties that Millie taught them: 'The Lily Livered Lobster' and 'Never Trust a Turbot'.

'Oh isn't this perfectly lovely!' said Millie. 'And a full moon!'

'And a full moon means a high tide or a low tide,' said a squeaky voice behind them.

The Daisy Drama Club jumped and turned round. There stood all twelve Turnarounds in nightshirts.

'And a low tide means razor clams.'

'And razor clams means supper!'

'You can dig them up when the tide is right out.'

'They leave little holes in the sand.'

'You can put little bits of salt on the holes to make them come up.'

'But if they don't come up you have to dig down as fast as you can with your fingers.'

'And pull them up before they burrow down faster than you can dig them up.'

'But sometimes the shells cut your fingers and you bleed all over the place.'

'That's because they are razor sharp.'

'Which is why they are called razor clams.'

'If you catch them you put them in a bucket.'

'Or just wash them in the stream by the beach then eat them raw.'

'Or cook them over a fire and the shells pop open.'

'We're going razor clam fishing tomorrow morning.'

'At low tide.'

'And a low tide means razor clams.'

'And razor clams means supper!'

The explanation about razor clams was going round for a second time. It was a habit of the Turnaround children that they had caught from Captain Turnaround. John interrupted.

'Can I come with you?'

'Doeth that mean we will have rathor clamth for our thupper too?' asked Susie in alarm.

'If you're lucky,' said Tom.

'But we've got to go back to our hammocks now,' said Tim.

'Before we go, why don't we tell them the lovely hammocktime story that Captain Turnaround told us tonight as our hammocktime story before we all got out of our hammocks again because we wanted to say goodnight to the DDC?' said Trixie.

'But the Daisy Drama Club already *know* the story because Captain Turnaround said it was the true story of the *real* lighthouse man that their play is about and that it was very kind of the Daisy Drama Club to be so thoughtful to have written a play about the first lighthouse man who is our great, great, great

113

many greats ago grandfather.'

'*Your* great, great, great many greats ago grandfather?' said Beaky surprised. How very odd! Grandpa Albert had said the story he based the play on was about *her* great, great, great many greats ago grandfather.

'Truffle *you* tell the story! You're the best storyteller of us all!'

Truffle smiled modestly and said he would if the Daisy Drama Club and John and Uncle Max and Millie would like him too.

'Oh yes please! How lovely!' cried Millie. 'I'll make some cocoa. There's nothing more wonderful than listening to a bedtime story - or hammocktime story - round a campfire under the stars with a full moon and the waves crashing and sipping hot cocoa!'

Truffle narrowed his eyes and began.

'This is the horribly gruesome tale of ghastly Pirate Grungrag, the one legged, one eyed pirate who killed his victims by poisoning their cocoa then chopping up their bodies for fish bait.'

Susie's eyes flew wide open in horror! This did not sound like a pleasant re-telling of *The Lighthouse Man and the Monster Eel*!

'One night a ferocious, fearsome storm blew up and the lighthouse man, who was our great grandad from lots of great grandads ago and who was the first lighthouse man on these rocks which was linked to the land only by a little ridge of rocks where he lived in a little hut with his little boy and little girl, spent all night outside in the storm turning and turning and turning with a light on his head because he had no lighthouse just like the lighthouse man in the play. Many ships were saved but the storm went on for seven whole days and nights. In the end the lighthouse man could not keep awake any longer and fell asleep in exhaustion in his little hut. That very night the gruesome Pirate Grungrag was sailing by in his ship *Black Bones*. A huge wave drove *Black Bones* onto these very rocks where it smashed to pieces and everyone drowned except for Grungrag. All the treasure he had on board was lost in the watery deep. Grungrag was mad with fury. Why had the lighthouse man not warned him? Spitting blood and loose teeth Grungrag dragged his horribly ripped open body up the jagged rocks where it ripped open a bit more. He heaved himself to the little hut, smashed open the

door and found the lighthouse man fast asleep and snoring. The rotten Grungrag made two steaming cups of cocoa and dropped three drops of deadly poison into one mug and left it by the sleeping, snoring lighthouse man. But Grungrag was as foolish as he was gruesome and got the mugs mixed up and drank the poisoned one himself. He staggered around in agony and just before he fell into the sea he left a curse ... 'He who sleeps on these rocks will be haunted by me!' Then he fell into the sea where he drowned and was nibbled away by an eel which soon became an enormous, monstrously monster sized eel because Grungrag was quite a gristly pirate and soon there was nothing left of Grungrag except his skull and crossbones. As for the lighthouse man, when he at last woke up the storm was gone and he was surprised to find a cup of cocoa on his bedside table. He couldn't remember making it but thought one of his children must have made it for him, even though they were still very young, so he drank it gratefully and then, because the storm had gone, went off to sleep again and slept soundly and never knew a thing ... although they do say if you listen carefully to the wind howling round the lighthouse it seems to say ... listen ...'

Truffle opened his eyes wide and said in a whispery, howly way ...

 117

'Grungrag is coming! Grungrag is coming!'

Susie was staring into her half drunk mug of cocoa in horror. 'You don't think ...'

'It's just a story of the story!' interrupted Cressida, knowing that poor Susie was frightened to death.

'For weeks afterwards,' went on Truffle, 'the lighthouse man was woken every night by the cry 'Grungrag is coming! Grungrag is coming!' so he decided to dig a secret tunnel from the rocky island to the shore so that he and his children could secretly escape if any gruesome pirates did turn up. But he kept it *very* secret so nobody knows were the passage is. And with all the treasure that kept washing up on the rocks the lighthouse man was able to build a lighthouse so he and his children could live more comfortably than just in a hut. And when he had built his fine lighthouse he decided to leave a riddle in code about the secret tunnel for future generations on the wall in our kitchen which he knew the pirates would not be able to crack because they are far too stupid. But the first lighthouse man had forgotten how clever he was himself and *nobody* ever since has been able to crack the code or solve the riddle. The end!'

The Turnaround children clapped their hands.

'That was a lovely story Truffle!'

'Lovely!'

The Turnaround children started yawning.

'Time for bed,' said Tadpole sleepily.

One by one the Turnaround children stood up, turned around and went back to the lighthouse to snuggle down in their hammocks.

'Time for us to go to bed too,' said Millie as cheerfully as she could. But even Millie was feeling a bit spooked ...

... so it was not surprising that during the night Susie, who was sharing a tent with Beaky, woke up suddenly.

'Beaky! Did you hear that?'

'What?'

'Grungrag is coming! Grungrag is coming!'

'No,' said Beaky going back to sleep and dreaming of lots and lots of great, great, great, lots of greats ago grandfathers swimming in the sea with cups of cocoa on their heads.

But Susie lay awake rigid with fear for the next hour. It was only by thinking of her mother, Mrs Theodora Whistle-White and wishing and wishing and wishing she was back home that she started to feel homesick, all tearful and achy inside which was just a tiny bit less terrible than feeling so frightened that she could hardly breathe. For the next hour Susie concentrated on missing her little cosy bed at home sobbing as quietly as she could into her pillow.

Finally, finally, she fell asleep.

Rehearsal on the Beach

The following morning after a breakfast of eggs cooked over the campfire by Millie, Cressida and Sophie read out the plan for the day.

'Ten o'clock. Rehearsal on Seaweed Beach.'

'Eleven o'clock. Enjoy the beach.'

'One o'clock. Go to *The Cave Theatre*'

'Two o'clock. Per ...'

'Good morning! Good morning!' interrupted Captain Turnaround flourishing a bit of paper. 'This is a map of *Castaway Bay* and the precise location of *The Cave Theatre*. Precisely precise. You can only get there by clambering round the rocky shore at low tide or by boat, by boat, at high tide.'

'So *The Cave Theatre* is actually on *Castaway Bay*,' said Abby looking at the map.

'You could say that! Say that again!' grinned Captain Turnaround. 'Trixie, Truffle and Teddy have been over at the crack of dawn and put up a big sign so you won't miss it. Oh no, you won't miss it. Not miss it at all! Tom will take you round in *Loosey Goosey* at one o'clock so you can all set up. Set up! Then he will go back and pick up the audience in *Loosey Goosey*. All meet at the flagpole. The flagpole.'

'It's very low tide now so Millie and I will stroll round to *Castaway Bay* while you rehearse,' said Uncle Max. 'John, do you want to come with us?'

John leapt at the chance. He could look out for seaside wildlife. He was making a list of all the things he had seen so far and so far he had seen millions of barnacles and mussels and whelks and five shore crabs and two hermit crabs and one starfish and caught some shrimps. And it was perfect timing to dig up razor clams. He couldn't wait to cook them in butter over the campfire for supper. Delicious!

It was half-past ten before the DDC set off for the beach. Somehow at the campsite everything seemed to take twice as long as normal.

'We're already behind schedule,' said Sophie, as they walked down the causeway towards Seaweed Beach, which was covered in holidaymakers enjoying the sunshine.

'Yes but we're only rehearsing things that went *wrong* yesterday,' added Cressida,' and it went really *well* yesterday so the rehearsal should be short.'

'Luckily Susie seemed to know all her lines and didn't seem at all worried about the audience in the end,' added Sophie, 'so we needn't worry about her missing the rehearsal this morning. But I can't think why she is so tired.'

As hard as they tried the DDC had not been able to wake up Susie so they had left her fast asleep in her tent.

'You guard her,' said Alice to Wolfgang. 'When she wakes up bring her down to the beach.'

Wolfgang snarled and flopped down in front of Susie's tent. He would guard Susie with his life!

Pickle meanwhile was already at work.

Toffee, Tadpole and Trousers had untied him from the Pirate's Ear Ring and trotted off to sell tickets for the afternoon's performance at *The Cave Theatre*.

'Let's go over to the rocks where it's a bit more private,' said Sophie.

But as soon as they started rehearsing a pale and pasty looking boy and a pale and pasty looking girl

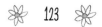

came and sat down right in front of them, chewing pink chews with their mouths wide open and staring and staring at the DDC.

'Just keep going,' whispered Cressida. 'Pretend nobody is watching.'

'Let's start with act one, scene five,' suggested Sophie. 'Princess Crabella has just been stolen away by Maximus and Queen Scuttlebucket finds King Fathom-Five-Deep fast asleep.'

Sophie started ...

```
QUEEN SCUTTLEBUCKET
    Stand back! Stand back! It's Super Queen!
    Super Queen! Super Queen!
    Kind to the good. Horrid to the mean!
    Super Queen! Super Queen!
```

'Why are *you* Super Queen?' shouted the chewing boy with his mouth open wider than ever and the chew going round faster and faster.

'You don't *look* like Super Queen,' said the chewing

girl who was wearing a bright pink swimming costume that matched her chew and who had sat down about an inch away from the rehearsal and kept pushing her hands through the soft sand and flipping it up at Sophie.

'That's because I'm not in costume,' said Sophie, surprised to be interrupted. 'This is a rehearsal.'

'What's a rehearsal?' shouted the boy, chewing and chewing.

'It's when you practise a play,' said Sophie.

'Don't you know it yet then?'

'Yes. We performed it yesterday.'

'So why do you need to practise?'

'Probably because it wasn't very good,' said the girl and she started to make a sandcastle and talk loudly and chew and spit all at the same time. 'I was in a play once and it was really good. Much better than this one. I was a blueberry and I had to sit on the wizard and squash him which I did and everyone laughed a lot. It was very funny. My mummy says I should do more acting but I don't like acting. I much prefer dancing. I'm really good at pointing my toe. Look I'll show you.'

The girl got up and started pointing her toe. Up, down. Up, down. Up, down. She flicked sand everywhere. Then she fell over and started crying.

'Just go away!' shouted Sophie losing her temper.

The girl cried louder.

A woman in a turquoise floaty dress ran over.

'Jessie! Jessie darling! Whatever is the matter? Don't cry honeybunch.'

'Mummy! Mummy! That horrid girl is being mean to me!' said Jessie bawling and pointing a sticky pokey finger at Sophie.

The turquoise lady turned to Sophie.

'You should be ashamed of yourself young lady! Come on Jessie. Don't cry bunnykins. I've got a perfectly lovely surprise for you. I've just bought some tickets from some very *charming* and delightfully *kind* children riding the sweetest little pony to a see a play later today at *Castaway Bay*. We have to go round by boat. That will be such a treat won't it pumpkin pie!'

And with that Jessie, the boy and their mother walked off.

Sophie was furious. She turned round. The rest of the DDC were rolling round on the beach *laughing!*

Sophie felt crosser still then decided not to be. She felt more determined than ever that the play would be really good, especially if Jessie and her awful family were going to be in the audience.

'Come on everyone,' she said. 'Let's get this play perfect!'

Harry took up where Jessie had interrupted.

```
KING FATHOM-FIVE-DEEP
    Super Queen? Super Queen?
    Am I seeing things or is this just a dream?
    Have you come to help me?
    I'm afraid I've lost my daughter in the water
    And my wife Queen Scuttlebucket,
    The old rotting wreck,
    Has got all snappy and cross
    And swum off looking like a bolshy barracuda
    Swallowed and spat out by a shark
    That's just chewed her!

QUEEN SCUTTLEBUCKET
    If you value your life
    You'll be more polite about your wife!
```

Sophie grinned. A small crowd of curious holidaymakers, who had gathered round to watch, started clapping. Sophie knew they would put on a good performance that afternoon and she could not *wait* to show the chewing, spitting, disgusting, bunnykins, pumpkin pie Jessie and her awful brother and ghastly turquoise mother just what the DDC could do!

Cracking the Code

Back at the campsite Susie woke up with a start.

'Beaky?'

No Beaky.

Susie unzipped the tent flap.

'Aaaah!'

Wolfgang was guarding Susie closely. He snarled at her, showing his razor white teeth and red gums. Susie shrieked and dived back into the tent, her heart pounding. She was trapped!

'Alith! Alith!' she shouted.

Silence.

Everyone had gone except Wolfgang!

Susie sat frozen in fear for half an hour. Every time she peeped out of the tent Wolfgang snarled. After an hour she thought that she would have to think of a plan. And then she did. She got dressed. Next she picked up her yellow and pink stripy pillow and threw it out of the tent as far as she could and shouted, 'Shoo! Shoo! Go and fetch! Stay ... away!'

Wolfgang yelped in delight. He dashed after the yellow and pink stripy thing and was about to bring it back to Susie when some soft white fluffy things started to float in the air. Feathers! This yellow and pink fluffy thing was not just a *thing*. It was a chicken!

 128

Something to have lots of fun with! Wolfgang threw it up in the air and caught it, then threw it up and caught it again and again.

'My pillow!' shrieked Susie.

Feathers were flying everywhere. Wolfgang had completely forgotten about Susie. Her plan had not included the total destruction of her pillow but at least this was her chance to escape! Remembering her mother was insistant that she must ...

...wash her face for one minute ...

... brush her teeth for five minutes ...

...brush her hair for three minutes... Susie grabbed her washbag to head for the washroom shed - but Wolfgang was leaping around with the pillow chicken right in front of the washroom door.

'I can't pothibly go into the wathroom with Wolfgang in the way but I can't pothibly go out in thith thtate,' thought poor Susie.

Although Susie could be feeble, she could also be brave and resourceful. Wolfgang was still going crazy with the chicken pillow so Susie took her chance and, on hands and knees, sneaked out of the tent. When she was far enough away from Wolfgang she stood up and made a dash for the lighthouse. Perhaps

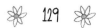

Mrs Turnaround would let her wash there.

Susie pushed open the door of the lighthouse kitchen and closed it behind her just in case Wolfgang was following her.

'Mithith Turnaround?' she called quietly at first.

'Mithith Turnaround?' she called loudly.

But there was nobody there.

'I'll jutht have to make do,' Susie decided.

Susie went over to the kitchen sink. She opened her washbag and got out her toothbrush and toothpaste and soap and flannel and hairbrush and propped her little mirror on the draining board. She looked in the mirror and washed her face then started to brush her teeth when she nearly choked in surprise. The funny code on the wall. She could read it!

She could read it in her mirror!

She turned to look at it directly and it looked like gobbledegook ... but in her mirror it was easy peasy!

Carefully she held up the mirror and slowly circled round the room reading every word. It said:

... not high but low and in you go ... at the end of the flow peep low ... not bottom but top and out you pop! ...

Susie had cracked the code!

She could not *wait* to tell the DDC!

Hurriedly she threw everything into her washbag, crept past the campsite so Wolfgang would not see her, then took off at top speed along the causeway to find the rest of the DDC. It wasn't long before she spotted them on the beach rehearsing, surrounded by a crowd of holidaymakers.

She ran as fast as she could over the sand, her heart pounding. Just as Super Queen Sophie was saying ...

```
Princess Crabella, wherever you are ...
Here comes your dear mama
```

Susie shouted at the top of her voice, 'I'm here! I'm here! I've cracked the code! I've cracked the code!'

The holidaymakers cheered. It was a most exciting play full of twists and turns. They would definitely get tickets for the performance.

Then someone said, 'Someone said there are not many tickets left for this afternoon's performance.'

It was only a rumour but it started a riot.

All the holidaymakers crowded in on the DDC trying to buy tickets.

'Four tickets please.'

'Six front row tickets over here!'

'Two and one for my auntie who can't hear so can we sit near the front too.'

'One ticket for myself and three for my nieces who are coming later so can you hold tickets for them - I would like to bag a good seat for them. They are only tichy tiny!'

Because lots of the holidaymakers were crowding round the DDC all the other holidaymakers decided something exciting was going on so they leapt off their deckchairs, forgot about their sandcastles, stopped digging holes, abandoned the ice-cream queue, dashed out of the sea and charged over to find out what all the commotion was about and when they found out that there were only a few tickets left for a play that they knew nothing about they decided they *must* have some tickets too.

'Five tickets here! Over here! Here!'

'I need three. But do you have an aisle seat? Uncle Bert has very long legs.'

'Four and room for a pushchair please.'

Someone pushed someone else by mistake and got an ice-cream in their face. A baby started crying. A boy threw a bucket of seawater over a man who was trying to barge to the front.

Sophie and Cressida and the rest of the DDC were surrounded!

'Quick,' said Cressie. 'Let me climb on your shoulders Sophie.'

Beaky and Abby and Alice and Lou helped Cressie onto Sophie's shoulders and Harry and Hen held onto Cressie's legs to steady her. Wobbling, Cressie stood up.

'Ladies and Gentlemen,' she said not sure what she was going to say next. In the distance she could see Pickle going at a fast trot along the beach with Toffee, Tadpole and Trousers bouncing about on his back and waving the Box Office sign. 'Tickets can be bought from the Pickle Box Office which is over there.'

Cressida pointed dramatically at Pickle.

The crowd turned.

They saw the sign saying *Box Office* and charged towards Pickle!

Toffee, Tadpole and Trousers, who were used to dealing with crowds, having such a large family, soon had them lined up in a Turnaround queue, which is in a circle and sold them tickets one by one. The performance at *The Cave Theatre* was going to be a sellout show!

Cressida jumped down from Sophie's shoulders and the DDC crowded round Susie who was still red in the face from running and excitement.

'I've cracked the secret code in the lighthouse kitchen!' she panted.

'Leaping liquorice!' said Harry and Hen. 'You're a genius!'

At that moment a grey hairy beast covered in feathers raced down the causeway, onto the beach and dived into the huddle of the DDC.

'Wolfgang! What have you been up to?' cried Alice.

'My code cracking ith really all down to Wolfgang,' said Susie and very bravely she put out a little hand and patted him lightly. 'If Wolfgang hadn't thought my pillow was a chicken I would never have made thuch an important dithcovery.'

'What does the code say?' asked Abby.

'That's the funny thing,' said Susie. 'Although I've cracked the code I have no idea what it meanth! Cracking the code doethn't mean to thay you have tholved the riddle! If we go and have another look I will thow you what I mean and you might be able to work it out.'

Cressida checked the time and the schedule.

'If we're quick we might just have time before we meet Trapdoor and Truck at the flagpole.'

'Yeth. It will only take a moment to *read* the code. It might take a bit longer to *tholve* the riddle,' Susie reassured them.

'Let's go!' said Sophie who loved a mystery.

The DDC raced down the causeway. The door to the lighthouse kitchen was open. Mrs Turnaround had just returned from a fishing trip and was inside, humming, whilst she flicked the silver scales off her catch, a large sea bass, with a blunt knife.

'Come in dears!' boomed Mrs Turnaround looking up and at the same time swopping the blunt knife for a dangerous looking shiny, razor thin, razor sharp one. 'I am just about to fillet this bass beauty for lunch. Are you all ravenous?'

'No thank you Mrs Turnaround,' said Sophie. 'But we would like to show you something. Or, at least, Susie would like to show you something.'

'Come in then! Come in!' said Mrs Turnaround. 'All the little Turnarounds are out busy preparing for this afternoon's performance so it will be nice to have some company.'

Sophie and Cressida felt a bit guilty that *they* were not preparing for this afternoon's performance but Susie had assured them it would only take a moment or two to *crack* the code if not to *solve* the riddle!

Susie got the mirror out of her washbag. 'Lucky I thtill have my wathbag with me,' she said mysteriously.

Susie held up the mirror.

'Look!' she said triumphantly turning round slowly.

Cressida, who was nearest, could see the writing on the wall reflected in Susie's mirror. She read it out aloud ...

... not high but low and in you go ... at the end of the flow peep low ... not bottom but top and out you pop! ...

'By the bones of a bouncing bass! You've cracked the code!' said Mrs Turnaround bouncing the half boned bass up and down on the kitchen table. 'You've cracked the code!'

'But what does it mean?' asked Abby.

Nobody could answer that.

'Let's write it down,' said Sophie. 'It might make more sense.'

'And we haven't got time to solve the riddle now anyway,' added Cressida. 'We have a play to perform!'

Cave Theatre Performance

The DDC raced to the campsite and stuffed all the costumes, make-up, props and lights into the tour chest and carried it down to the flagpole meeting place.

Uncle Max, Millie and John came rushing from the other direction having had a marvellous morning exploring *Castaway Bay*.

Trunk and Trapdoor arrived from the seaward direction in the *Loosey Goosey*, with Captain Turnaround Junior at the helm, and helped the DDC, Uncle Max, Millie, John and Wolfgang all aboard. Pickle declined to get on a boat again and stayed for some peaceful grazing at the campsite.

John, Millie and Uncle Max were all talking at once as the *Loosey Goosey* set out to sea.

'I dug up loads of razor clams for supper!'

'We found such a dear little crab scuttling about.'

'We nearly got cut off by the tide!'

But the DDC had even more exciting news.

'Susie's cracked the code!'

'But we can't solve the riddle!'

'Look!'

Cressida handed over the piece of paper with the riddle written on it for Uncle Max, Millie and John to have a look.

'Oh you are clever!' said Millie. 'But what does it mean?'

'We've got to work that out,' shouted Cressida above the roar of the engine.

John was looking carefully at the riddle and his heart started racing. After searching for razor clams he had explored *Castaway Bay* and made quite a discovery himself. Could it be linked to the riddle? He would soon find out!

Loosey Goosey ran alongside a small wooden jetty just off *Castaway Bay*. Everyone disembarked and carried the tour chest onto the beach.

The DDC gasped.

Further up the beach was a large cave. Above the cave was an enormous sign saying *Cave Theatre*. Around the cave were little Turnarounds busy rigging up a stage with planks of driftwood, hanging up bunting, putting up little tables selling drinks and sweets and ice-creams and programmes, making little sandcastles for people to sit on and putting up screens saying *private-make-up* and *private-changing rooms*.

'Leaping liquorice!' said Harry and Hen together as Captain Turnaround Junior left in *Loosey Goosey* to pick up the audience.

Trunk and Trapdoor handed John some lanterns.
'Lighting,' said Trunk.

John was delighted. His lights were no good in a
cave with nowhere to plug them in. He carried the
lanterns up the beach. Uncle Max helped him light
them and set them up on rocky shelves. They glinted
against the black rock and looked exciting and
atmospheric. And, thought John, they were just what
he needed for exploring the back of the cave ...

On the beach Sophie and Cressida gathered the
DDC round for a meeting. Out at sea *Loosey Goosey*
was already rounding the headland again bringing
the audience across to *The Cave Theatre*.

'Looks like we've got a full house,' said Sophie.

'Don't you mean full beach!' added Abby giggling.

'A full beach then,' said Sophie. 'The main thing is to speak up loudly so the audience can hear. It's not going to be easy with the wind and the sea and we've got to show chewing Jessie and her ghastly family that we can put on a really good show.'

The audience was landing on the jetty.

'Break a leg!' said Cressie.

'Break a leg!' said the DDC.

Getting changed and putting on make-up behind the screens was not easy. Abby was just putting on her Cornet costume when the screen blew down. When Harry and Hen were getting changed chewing Jessie and her pale and pasty brother kept peeping round to have a look. And Lou found it very difficult to keep the sand out of her make-up box.

But by two o'clock the cast were ready and the audience were waiting. A horn sounded out at sea and *Loosey Goosey* came round the rocks with a final boatload of audience.

As Abby had thought, it was a full beach!

Millie sends Postcard No 4

My Dear Creaky Old People,

Oh just imagine! The Daisy Drama Club are performing on a beach! The stage is in a cave and the lights are lanterns. It all looks so pretty! I do wish you were here. Oh that nasty Maximus the Monster Eel is about to capture Cornet. I do find this bit upsetting. Poor little boy! But I know he will be rescued in the end by his sister and the brave lighthouse man who will hypnotise the monster but you never know until you know. I hope you are keeping warm and eating healthily and not forgetting to go out for a nice walk each day and if you do don't forget to put on your ... here Mille ran out of room so she finished quickly ... Lots of love and hugs and kisses Millie xxxxx

SEAWARD ~ ON ~ SEA
ICE CREAMS
WHERE EVERY DAY IS A HOLIDAY

Nearly Solving the Mystery

Whilst the first act was going on, John took one of the lanterns and crept to the back of the cave.

Yes! Just as he had thought.

Earlier in the day, when he had visited *Castaway Bay* with Uncle Max and Millie, John had gone alone into the cave to look for unusual creatures. He had had to feel along the cave walls because it was too dark to see. He had felt all sorts of whelks and barnacles and limpets and had gone deeper and deeper into the pitch black. Suddenly he came to a dead end. The back of the cave. He was just about to turn round when his hand felt something hard and smooth. He felt the shape. Long and triangular. Next to it he could feel something wooden. Wooden planks set in the rock face. Could it be a door hinge? ... and a door? He ran his hands excitedly up and down, from side to side ... another hinge

... a lock ... It must be a little wooden door set into the cave wall. And then his hands fell upon a handle. Excitedly he pulled. But the door was firmly locked. There must be a key. Hurriedly he felt all around but found nothing.

Uncle Max called into the cave.

'John! Are you there? Time to go!'

'Go! Go! Go! Go!' echoed around the cave.

John clambered back out of the cave. He promised himself to return later with a light and find the key. Here he was now with a lantern. And he was sure that the little door must be something to do with the lighthouse riddle!

The lantern flickered as he went deeper into the cave, right to the end. There was the little door but where was the key?

What did the riddle say? ... *not high, but low and in you go* ... That could mean going *in* to something which could be the cave at *low* tide not *high*. The tide was turning now so he could still get into the cave but at high tide the seawater would flow right to the end of the cave. That was the next clue ... *at the end of the flow peep low* ... That's it! He would look for the key somewhere low down, right at the back of the cave.

John held out the lantern and ...

... leapt out of his skin in horror!

Something had grabbed his shoulder!

'Waaaaah!'

John swung the lantern round lighting up a face painted in horizontal stripes.

Pirate Grungrag!

'Waaaaaah!'

'John! What are you doing?'

It was Beaky!

'Beaky! You scared me! I thought you were Pirate Grungrag back from his grave! What are *you* doing?'

'I had to come backstage which is back into the cave and I saw a light so I thought I would investigate. What are *you* doing?'

'Look Beaky.'

Beaky gasped in amazement as John held up his lantern and showed her the little door.

'It's locked. There must be a key but I can't find it.'

John's lantern went out.

'Bloomin' barnacles! I can't see a thing!'

'I have the solution,' said Beaky and she turned on the lighthouse man's light on her head which turned round and round.

Beaky's light went round and round so every other second or two Beaky and John could see which was better than not being able to see at all.

'It's all to do with the riddle in the lighthouse,' said John. 'Remember ...*at the end of the flow peep low* ...'

John and Beaky got on their hands and knees and looked in all the little cracks and crevices for a key. Something suddenly glinted in the light of Beaky's light. Something hidden low down in a crack in the rock. John squeezed his hand in and his fingers closed on something cold and hard. He pulled it out.

The key!

It shone, bright and golden in Beaky's light.

Beaky gasped in amazement.

'Quick! Let's see if it works!'

John put the key in the lock and turned.

Click!

'Beaky! Beaky! Are you there?'

It was Sophie calling. Sophie had seen the flashing light towards the back of the cave and had stumbled towards it, urgently looking for Beaky.

'HURRY BEAKY! We are on act two, scene four. You're on stage *any second*!'

Trapped!

Beaky forgot about solving riddles and secret doors and hurried back to the stage. Without Beaky it was pitch black in the cave so John put the key in his pocket and followed. He would return later with another lantern to solve the riddle once and for all!

Beaky led the way with her on-off, on-off, on-off light and turning and turning dashed onto the stage just in time!

```
MAXIMUS THE MONSTER EEL
    Ha! Ha! Ha! Oooooh!

ANGELICA and CORNET
    Dad?

LACHLAN THE LIGHTHOUSE MAN
    Bloomin' barnacles there you are!
    Forgive me. I'm such a bloomin' bad dad.
    Hopeless! Neglectful! A fool!
    I feel so bad turning my back on you again ...
    ... and again ... and again ...
    And so careless ... bloomin' losing you again.
    So it being calm up above
    And no danger of wrecks
    I thought I'd better come
    And have a look for you under the seas
    - below decks.
    I tried some of the ice-cream
    Cornet had only licked half
    And it turned me into a fish,
    So I could swim to find you - my dearest wish!
```

ANGELICA
  Dad keep turning!

LACHLAN THE LIGHTHOUSE MAN
  Keep turning? That's the problem.
  I can't stop turning whatever the location.
  Turning is my vocation!

ANGELICA
  Dad! You hero!
  Your turning has hypnotised
  The monstrous monster of the deep
  Sent him into a deep sleep!
  He's in a trance! This is our chance
  To make him obey and do what we say!
  Turn him to good from bad
  Make him - and us - happy not sad!

Even the chewy, spitty Jessie cheered. The
lighthouse man was a hero! Sophie and Cressida felt
tiptop. The play was going better than they could
have imagined.

That is until the sky darkened and a few large drops of rain started to fall. The rain drops became heavier and heavier and the audience made a dash for cover - round behind the stage and inside the cave!

The DDC were used to unexpected challenges by now. They simply turned round and completed the play with the audience on the *other* side of the stage.

Outside the wind was howling and the rain beat down but the DDC actors continued, performing as true professionals right to the final curtain!

```
CORNET
    I suppose you could say
    That although eels make rotten meals
    They make great friends ...

ANGELICA
    ... and that, folks,
    Is how this fishy tale ends!
    Waaaaaah!
```

As Cressida delivered the final line a crash of thunder made her jump out of her skin! The audience applauded, clapping hard, impressed by the dramatic sound effects, but when a flash of lightning lit up the beach *everyone* jumped out of their skin!

Children started crying ...

    ... mums turned pale ...

        ... dads turned pale ...

Outside the rain was falling heavily and the sea had turned from a calm millpond to a churning mass of frothing waves! Captain Turnaround Junior ran out to the *Loosey Goosey* but a huge wave had ripped the ring that she was tied to off the jetty and she was floating out to sea! There was no other way off *Castaway Bay* ... and the tide was still coming in!

Captain Turnaround Junior ran back up the beach to the cave where everyone was sheltering from the rain. He just got there when a huge wave roared into the cave sending everyone rushing further back into the cave for cover. There followed another wave and another.

The DDC and the audience were pushed deeper and deeper into the cave.

They were trapped!

Escape!

Sophie and Cressida looked at each other in dismay. It was getting chaotic.

'I want to go home! Right now!' came a squeaky whine that made Sophie's heart sink.

Jessie.

But to Sophie and Cressida's amazement John's voice, from the depth of the cave, boomed out loud and clear ...

'We hope you have enjoyed the play. We now have a very special treat for you! Follow me. And bring a lantern if you can find one.'

John! What on earth was he up to?

John was gambling on an idea that he had.

He just hoped he was right!

'Beaky turn on your light and come to the back of the cave. Quick!'

Beaky, with her flashing light on her head for others to follow, followed John and his lantern to the back of the cave.

John took the key out of his pocket and shone his lantern light onto the secret door. He turned the key in the lock.

Click!

John pulled on the door handle. There was the

squeaky, creaky sound of an ancient door opening.

The door opened into pitch blackness.

John swung his lantern inside.

Yes! Just as he thought.

There was a tunnel cut into the rock.

'Everyone follow me!'

John held up his lantern and squeezed through the door, leading the way. It was dark and cold in the passageway. Icy water drops dripped onto his head. Behind him followed the Daisy Drama Club, the audience, the Turnaround children and bringing up the rear were Uncle Max and Millie.

'Isn't this exciting!' said Millie. 'Oh I do love an adventure!'

Millie started singing *The Lily Livered Lobster.* Slowly but surely everyone joined in, even the most nervous of the adventurers.

'John,' whispered Sophie to her brother. 'How do you know where we are going?'

'I don't *exactly*,' admitted John. 'It's just an idea.'

At that moment the tunnel came to an abrupt halt. A dead end! Everyone squashed up and they suddenly all seemed to be squeezed into a very small space.

'I don't like it!' Jessie whined.

'I don't like it!

I don't like it!

I don't like it!

I don't like it!

I don't like it!'

echoed her voice far back into the tunnel.

'John,' hissed Sophie anxiously. 'It's a dead end!'

'Wait! I'm thinking ...'

What was the last line of the riddle?

'*...not bottom but top and out you pop! ...*'

John held up his lantern and looked up.

There it was above him.

A trapdoor!

'Here we are!' he cried cheerily. 'We just need to open the trapdoor.'

But the trapdoor was too high to reach.

'Sophie, stand still.'

 153

With the help of Cressida and the rest of the DDC John stood on Sophie's shoulders, pushed open the trapdoor and heaved himself up and disappeared.

Everyone held their breath.

'What can you see?' called up Sophie.

'Pass me a lantern,' called back John.

Sophie passed up a lantern. From its light John could see he was in a strange circular room with shelves all around, stacked with all sorts of dried fish and seaweed and jars of winkles and limpets and barrels of cockles and mussels. In the middle was a circular staircase going up to another trapdoor.

Leaning against the shelves was a ladder used for climbing up and down to reach the stores. Perfect!

John lowered the ladder down to Sophie.

Immediately everybody started climbing up and pouring up into the store room.

'Where are we?' asked Abby in amazement.

But John was already making his way up the circular steps. He threw open the trapdoor at the top and cried out, 'Yippee! Just as I thought!'

He was in the kitchen of Seaward-on-Sea Lighthouse!

Captain Turnaround and Mrs Turnaround were sitting at the kitchen table, their heads buried in their hands, sobbing. They looked up when John burst in -

then burst into tears again.

'Our children! Lost at sea! Lost at sea!'

At that moment the Turnaround children came charging up the circular steps and hurled themselves into the kitchen.

'We're home!'

'We've found the secret tunnel!'

'We found it from the *other* end!'

'We're starving!'

Mrs Turnaround was so surprised to see them that she fainted.

'We thought you had drowned!' said Captain Turnaround. 'When the storm came up we saw *Loosey Goosey* being tossed around at sea. We were so worried that you might fall out. But Pickle was so brave! He leapt out of the campsite and swam out and grabbed the rope of *Loosey Goosey* in his mouth and towed it back to shore. But when we looked inside it was empty. No children! We thought you were lost at sea!'

'Oh no!' said Tom Turnaround. 'When the storm came up *Loosey Goosey* was ripped off the jetty ...'

'But John solved the riddle'

'And here we are!'

'Safe and sound!'

'Safe and sound!'

Razor Clam Supper

Back at the campsite Millie and Uncle Max lit the campfire and the DDC helped John cook their razor clam supper.

'You are a hero!' said Cressida to John.

'For rescuing us, not for the razor clam supper,' added Lou looking in horror at the slimy white thing on her plate.

'I with I had a brother like you,' said Susie. 'You're tho lucky Thophie.'

For the millionth time Beaky thought how lucky anyone was who had a brother *or* a sister. Lucky Sophie, lucky Harry and Hen, lucky Turnarounds!

She sighed and ate her razor clams. At least they didn't taste as disgusting as they looked.

In the middle of the night some of the DDC were awoken by lots of noisy tiptoeing and loud quiet whispers. Mrs Turnaround was saying loudly, as quietly as she could ...

'I'm so sorry. I don't seem to have a booking for Bluebell House but I'm sure we can make room for you if you squeeze your tents over by the wall.'

In the morning when the DDC woke up they noticed two more tents had appeared. Coming from inside were all sorts of snorings and snufflings.

But the DDC were too busy to investigate. They still had one more performance to put on.

Sophie and Cressida read out the plan for the day.

'Ten o'clock. Rehearsal on Seaweed Beach.'

'Eleven o'clock. Enjoy the beach.'

'One o'clock. Go to *Turnaround Theatre.*'

'Two o'clock. Per ...

'Good morning! Good morning!' interrupted Captain Turnaround. 'Today you must be ready at the flagpole at half past one! Not so far today. Today!'

'Captain Turnaround,' said Abby, 'where is the *Turnaround Theatre?*'

'Right here of course!' said Captain Turnaround turning around. 'At Seaward-on-Sea Lighthouse. Where else *could* it be?'

Abby looked but she could not see a theatre.

'Let's go down to the beach and rehearse,' suggested Cressida. 'I'm sure it will all be made clear when we wait by the flagpole.'

Cressida and Sophie were starting to enjoy the surprise of not knowing exactly where they would be performing next.

The DDC set off for the beach. Meanwhile the Turnaround children were busy going up and down, up and down the secret tunnel to *Castaway Bay* and bringing back the stage and props and costumes and bunting. They could have gone on *Loosey Goosey* but were so excited by the secret passage that they kept wanting to go backwards and forwards like little moles.

When everything was back at Seaward-on-Sea Lighthouse they started building the *Turnaround Theatre* - on the rocks round the lighthouse itself!

First, they built a stage from planks of driftwood.

Second, they took out all the benches from the kitchen and chairs from the bedrooms for seating. Because the benches were semi-circular they made the perfect seating for a theatre in the round.

Thirdly, they were up and down ladders hanging up bunting.

Fourthly, they carried out little tables from the house for selling drinks and sweets and ice-creams.

 159

Fifthly, they put up a sign saying *programmes*.

Sixthly, they put up screens with signs saying *private - make-up* and *private - changing rooms*.

Seventhly, they put all the props and costumes back in the tour chest.

Eighthly, Captain Turnaround hung a big flag out of the top of the lighthouse saying,

'Turnaround Theatre! Theatre!'

The DDC on the beach saw the flag fluttering in the breeze.

'Look!' shouted Abby. 'The *Turnaround Theatre!*'

The DDC could not wait for one o'clock so ran down the causeway to have a look at the third theatre of their tour.

'A theatre in the round!' breathed Sophie, thrilled.

'We are going to have to adapt our performance,' said Cressie. 'We will have audience all around us so we need to make sure we act in all directions.'

'We also need to make sure we have all our props back from *Castaway Bay*,' added Sophie.

Meanwhile Lou had been checking the costumes. During the escape costumes had been caught on the jagged rocks.

'Super Queen's cloak is all torn!'

'King Fathom-Five-Deep's crown is coming apart!'

'And look at Maximus' top!' added Susie. 'Thredth!

Abtholute thredth! Thall I help you mend them Lou?'

Lou, Beaky and Susie were soon cutting, snipping and stitching whilst Harry and Hen re-stuck bits onto the Brother Nit Wit Detector Kit. Alice used a spare driftwood plank and painted a magnificent poster on it advertising the play and Abby went down to the beach with Bertie, Pickle, Toffee, Tadpole and Trousers to sell tickets.

Cressida and Sophie, amazingly found they had some free time!

'I've got the perfect idea,' said Sophie. 'Come with me!'

'Not another mystery,' said Cressida.

'Not a mystery - a treat!' said Sophie as she led the way down the causeway and over to the

Seward-on-Sea beach cafe. The girls bought a large vanilla cornet each and went to sit on the rocks where they could dip their toes into the rock pools as they licked their ice-creams.

The sun was warm and the sea sparkled.

The mix of lazing about by the sea and the shivery thrill of another performance about to happen was what going on tour to the seaside was all about!

Turnaround Theatre

At one fifty a large audience had gathered at the flagpole. By two o'clock the audience was sitting in the round at the *Turnaround Theatre* waiting for the performance of *The Lighthouse Man and the Monster Eel* to begin.

Lou stepped onto the stage.

MERMAN
```
    Come. Take my hand and together
    We'll slip beneath the breaking waves,
    Under the swaying waters of endless blue ...
```

'Wait!' came a sudden shout.

It was Mrs Turnaround.

'Wait! Six old doddery campers came last night especially to see the play. They said they travelled miles and miles and miles to get here so we simply can't start without them!'

'Six very old very doddery people?' asked a man in the third row.

'Six,' confirmed Mrs Turnaround.

'I saw six old people playing cricket on *Castaway Bay* at low tide,' said the man in the third row.

'But the tide has *turned* now,' said Mrs Turnaround.

'It's too late to come back over the rocks.'

'They might be trapped!'

'We must rescue them!'

'I wonder,' said Millie to Uncle Max. 'You don't think they are my five *creaky* old people do you?'

'Impossible! Mrs Turnaround said *six*.'

'Oh but Max! I can't bear to think it *might* be them or people just like them! We must go and find out!'

Captain Turnaround Junior brought *Loosey Goosey* round to the jetty and the rescue party, which was the

the DDC, John, Millie, Uncle Max, the Turnaround children, Captain and Mrs Turnaround and the entire audience, boarded. Nobody wanted to be left out.

'Everyone keep a sharp eye out for dodderers!'

Everyone leaned out looking at the shore for any sign of movement.

The *Turnaround Theatre* was deserted.

As the *Loosey Goosey* disappeared round the headland towards *Castaway Bay* the kitchen door of Seaward-on-Sea Lighthouse opened and out came five doddery old people and one not so doddery old person. They blinked in the sunlight.

'I say! What a stroke of luck!'

'That passageway from the beach has led us straight to the theatre.'

'And I thought we were going to be late.'

'But where is everyone else?'

'Let's sit down and wait.'

'At least we will have jolly good seats.'

'I'll go and buy us all ice-creams until the performers and audience turn up,' said the less doddery one.

So the five doddery old people sat down and waited, enjoying the sunshine and the less doddery one skipped down the causeway to the beach cafe.

Meanwhile the search and rescue team had kept a sharp eye out on the cliffs and the rocks but saw nothing.

'Let's turn back,' said Captain Turnaround Junior.

'Oh no!' cried Millie. 'Please let us go as far as *Castaway Bay!*'

So the rescue team ploughed on to *Castaway Bay.*

And then they saw it!

A red sunhat decorated with white and yellow daises bobbing along on the water.

Captain Turnaround Junior fished it out with his boathook. Millie gave a little scream!

'It's exactly the same as Miss Windrush's sunhat, one of my five creaky old people! You don't think ... oh!'

Millie burst into tears and buried her face in Uncle Max's beard!

Loosey Goosey floated about looking for more clues but none could be found. They chugged back to the

causeway. As they rounded the point they could quite clearly see the *Turnaround Theatre* ...

... and six old people sitting on the front row licking ice-creams.

'My creaky old people,' breathed Millie, wiping away her tears.

'And Grandpa Albert!' added Beaky astonished.

The six old people waved at the *Loosey Goosey* and carried on licking their ice-creams.

'Hurray! Here they come. I wonder why everyone is so late?'

'I say! I think someone has found my hat!'

Millie leapt off the *Loosey Goosey* and hugged each creaky old person in turn.

'Millie dear, we got your postcards.'

'We just had to come.'

'We just couldn't bear to miss out.'

'So here we are.'

'Grandpa Albert bought us in Miranda the milk float so it took a very long time which is why we were so late arriving at the campsite last night.'

Beaky hugged Grandpa Albert.

'I'm so glad you are here,' she said. 'There's so much to tell you but not now - we have a show to put on!'

Performing *The Lighthouse Man and the Monster Eel* in the round suited the play perfectly. At the final bow the audience clapped and cheered.

What a performance!

What a play!

What a cast!

Grandpa Albert was so excited he stood up and yelled, 'Fantasticalicas!'

'By Neptune's barnacled beard!' cried Captain Turnaround swivelling his head round at 100 knots to have a look at the person who owned the voice that had shouted *'Fantasticalicas!'* 'Is that *you* Albert?'

'Arthur?' said Albert, staring in astonishment at Captain Turnaround. 'Is that *you* Arthur. My little baby brother *Arthur*?'

'My oldest ancient brother *Albert*?'

Beaky was looking from one to the other.

'It is you! We haven't seen each other for years. Years and years and years.'

'No. I lost touch with all our brothers and sisters except our oldest sister, ancient Ethel who lives up north.'

'And I am in touch with our youngest sister, little Enid who lives down south. Down south.'

'And I told Ethel about the fantasticalicas DDC!'

'And Enid must have told Ethel. Told Ethel.'

'Who told you.'

'Who told me.'

'So you wrote to the fantasticalicas DDC to invite them to the Seaward-on-Sea Festival!'

'I did! I did!'

'If you are brothers,' said Beaky, her heart beating wildly, 'that makes the Turnaround children my ...'

Beaky was looking from Albert to Arthur. If Grandpa Albert and Captain Turnaround were brothers did that make the Turnaround children her brothers and sisters?

No! That was quite wrong.

Not brothers and sisters.

Cousins?

No! Not cousins ...

... that made the Turnaround children her ...

WHAT?

'Your first cousins once removed,' whispered one of the doddery old people. 'I'm a genealogist. I know these things.'

'Removed from what?' asked Beaky, still confused. Then, she thought, it doesn't really matter. Having a whole load of first cousins removed from *anything* was nearly as good as having a whole load of brothers and

sisters.

In fact, thought Beaky, hugging ...
first cousin once removed Tom,
first cousin once removed Tim,
first cousin once removed Trixie,
first cousin once removed Truffle,
first cousin once removed Teddy,
first cousin once removed Trumpet,
first cousin once removed Triangle,
first cousin once removed Trapdoor,
first cousin once removed Truck,
first cousin once removed Toffee,
first cousin once removed Tadpole,
... and first cousin once removed Trousers
... and being hugged by ...
first cousin once removed Trousers,
first cousin once removed Tadpole,
first cousin once removed Toffee,
first cousin once removed Truck,
first cousin once removed Trapdoor,
first cousin once removed Triangle,
first cousin once removed Trumpet,
first cousin once removed Teddy,
first cousin once removed Truffle,
first cousin once removed Trixie,
first cousin once removed Tim,

...and first cousin once removed Tom ... it was ...

fantasticalicas!

Final Turnaround

Captain Turnaround and Mrs Turnaround invited Uncle Max, Millie and her creaky old people into the lighthouse for tea. Captain Turnaround was keen to show his brother Albert *The Complete and Total History of Seaward-on-Sea Lighthouse*.

The Turnaround children dismantled the *Turnaround Theatre*.

The DDC and John took down the tents and packed up the tour minibus.

Cressida got out her now very tatty list of *Things To Take On Tour* and started to tick things off in reverse.

In the end they got tired and just stuffed everything into the tour box as fast as they could and tied the tour box on top of the tour minibus.

Then they rolled up the tents and put them into the tour minibus.

Then they picked up all the bits and pieces they had left on the campsite and put them in the tour minibus.

Then Alice tied her big poster she had painted on the driftwood on top of the tour box which was on top of the tour minibus.

Then the tour box and the tour minibus were full

and ready to go and the DDC and the Turnaround children were too hot and too tired to do another thing ...

... except for one thing ...

The sun was shining and the afternoon was hot.

The DDC and John put on their swimming things.

Beaky's first cousins once removed put on their swimming things.

Wolfgang and Pickle and Bertie did not put on their swimming things.

Then they all stood on the jetty and with a...

ONE!
   TWO!
      THREE!
         WOOF! WOOF!
            NEIGH! NEIGH!
               SQUEAK! SQUEAK!

...everyone jumped into the sea.

'Race you to that buoy!' yelled Sophie to Cressida.

The girls swam out as fast as they could which was slowly as it was choppy and they were trying to talk at the same time as swim.

 173

When they got to the buoy they bobbed around holding on tight to get their breath back. Closer to the shore they could see the rest of the DDC and Turnarounds splashing and shrieking in the water.

'I thought that when we set up the DDC we would just put plays on and it would be simple,' said Sophie.

'But it's much more exciting when it's full of unknown twists and turns,' added Cressida.

They bobbed about a bit longer thinking of all the surprising, unexpected, strange and weird and wonderful things that had happened to them since they had received the mystery letter from Captain Turnaround at the start of the summer holidays.

'What do you think is the best thing about coming on tour?' asked Cressida, trying to think what she thought *was* the best thing about coming on tour.

'Acting in three peculiar theatres?'

'Solving a riddle?'

'Beaky getting a new family?'

Before they could decide on the very best bit a tremendous bang from the shore made them leap out of their skins. Trumpet had let off the cannon again and an enormous banner shot out across the bay ...

'The Seaward-on-Sea Festival is over! Thank you to the fantasticalicas Daisy Drama Club. Fantasticalicus!'

And then a most extraordinary thing happened.

All the holidaymakers on the beach stopped eating their ice-creams and digging their holes and patting their sandcastles and eating their picnics and putting up their deckchairs and stood up and clapped.

Then spitting, chewing Jessie shouted,

'Three cheers for the Daisy Drama Club.'

The whole beach cheered.

Sophie and Cressida grinned at each other. This must be the very best moment! And it also meant that for Sophie and Cressida bobbing around on the buoy there was just one thing left to think about ...

... the next production for the Daisy Drama Club!

Did you know ...

... you really CAN put on

the Daisy Drama Club's

monster eel play

Just email

scripts@beetleheart.co.uk

and we'll send you all the info!

Love from the

daisy drama club

www.daisydramaclub.co.uk

by belinda roberts

BOOKS

daisy drama club

www.daisydramaclub.co.uk

- Stage Fright! - Daisy Drama Club
- Spotlight! - Daisy Drama Club
- On Tour - Daisy Drama Club

- Mr Darcy Goes Overboard
  (Sourcebooks)

PLAYS

- Angelica ... and the Monstrous, Monster of the Deep *
  (Samuel French)

- Scrooge! *
- Beetleheart *
- Rose! ... and the Wicked Wolfee *
- Christmas Candy *
- Daydream Believer *
- OTMA's Glory
- Vivaldi's Angels
- Starry Night
- Pride, Pop and Prejudice

mini-scripts

- The Frog Princess
- Creation • Jonah • The Real Mother

(* performed by the original Daisy Drama Club)

www.beetleheart.co.uk

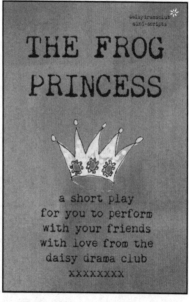

daisy drama club
mini-scripts

THE FROG PRINCESS

a short play
for you to perform
with your friends
with love from the
daisy drama club
xxxxxxxx

mini-scripts
www.daisydramaclub.co.uk

 180